# ROXY & JONES

## THE CURSE OF THE GINGERBREAD WITCH

# ROXY & JONES

## THE CURSE OF THE GINGERBREAD WITCH

### ANGELA WOOLFE

WALKER
BOOKS

First published in Great Britain 2021 by Walker Books Ltd
87 Vauxhall Walk, London SE11 5HJ

2 4 6 8 10 9 7 5 3 1

This book has been typeset in Berkeley Oldstyle

Printed and bound by CPI Group (UK) Ltd, Croydon CR0 4YY

British Library Cataloguing in Publication Data:
a catalogue record for this book is available from the British Library

ISBN 978-1-4063-9138-1

www.walker.co.uk

For Lara and Josh,
with all my love

## LATE AT NIGHT,
## THE DECONTAMINATION ZONE...

Roxy Humperdinck gripped the tiny piece of grit in her hand as if it was a life raft thrown to her in the middle of a treacherous ocean.

In her head, she was already trying out the words of the magic-blocking spell she'd learned only three days ago from Frankie, her friend Jones's fairy godmother. *Exodus Magicam*, she said to herself.

*Repeat this over and over*, she thought, and it might just do the trick. *Exodus Magicam... Exodus Magicam...*

Mrs Smith – the senior Ministry official who'd come to the hospital wing of the Decontamination Zone for the express purpose of putting Roxy back under the False Memory Enchantment – was sitting beside Roxy's bed, gazing down at her. The Ministry official's eyes, through the lenses of her pebble-thick glasses, were the pale blue of a summer sky.

"Close your eyes now," said Mrs Smith. "And try to relax."

Roxy could not have been further from relaxed.

This was it. This was the moment of truth. This was when her plan would be put into action.

If her plan was even worthy of the term *plan*.

It had only been a few days ago that Roxy had even learned of the existence of the False Memory Enchantment. This was the spell that kept everyone in complete ignorance about the truth of Illustria's secret past as a magical kingdom of fairies and witches – and, most importantly of all, a place where fairytales had really happened. Roxy's eyes had been opened to the truth by her new friend Jones, a treasure hunter for ancient magical artefacts with whom Roxy had been on the most incredible adventure. However, it was thanks to that adventure and an encounter with the spirit of the evil Queen that Roxy had ended up here in the Decontamination Zone. Roxy was silently pretty proud that she had defeated the evil Queen's spirit by turning it into a giant vegan muffin. But it meant that Mrs Smith, a senior official from the Ministry Overseeing, Organizing Or Occasionally Opposing Hocus-Pocus (MOOOOOH) had to come and put Roxy under the enchantment again. It did not do for the Ministry to let regular people know the truth. They needed Roxy to forget everything she had learned on her adventure with Jones: the magic, the fairytales…

But Roxy was planning to hang on to her memories. Roxy was hoping to block the enchantment.

She *seriously* wished Jones was here right now.

"Remind me once more of your name, child," said Mrs Smith.

"Roxy." She swallowed, hard. "Roxy Humperdinck."

"Ah, yes. Gretel Humperdinck's sister. How nice." Mrs Smith's eyes closed behind her pebbly glasses. *"Let this sweet forgetting charm Roxy's restless mind becalm,"* she intoned.

*Exodus Magicam*, thought Roxy. *Exodus Magicam, Exodus Magicam…*

She could feel the tiny piece of grit nestled in her hand starting to grow warm. She was expecting this. When she had (kind of accidentally, to be honest) turned the evil Queen into a vegan muffin, the magical Witching Stone she had used to perform the spell had turned warm. And this tiny fragment had come from that exact Stone.

*"Wasted wisdom cease to be,"* continued Mrs Smith. *"Magic fly from memory…"*

*Exodus … Magicam … Exodus … Magicam…* Roxy

whispered inside her head, gripping the piece of Stone tighter than ever. *Exodus … Magicam…*

"… *simula mnimini incantex!*" Mrs Smith finished, with a flourish.

There was a silence.

"Well!" Mrs Smith opened her eyes and looked down at Roxy. Those lenses really were the thickest Roxy had ever seen; her eyesight must be awful. "How are you feeling?"

Roxy let out all her breath in a rush. "I feel fine." She gazed back at Mrs Smith, eyes wide as those of a newborn. "Is there any reason I shouldn't feel fine, Mrs… I'm sorry, I don't think I know your name?"

The Ministry official's lips curved upwards in an imitation of a smile. "I'm Mrs Smith, child. You've had a little bump on the head. A skiing accident. *Terribly* dangerous sport." She got to her feet. "Rest now, and I'm sure your sister will be in to check on you soon."

Roxy settled back against the pillows and watched Mrs Smith walking towards the door.

Then the woman stopped, and turned.

For a brief but heart-stopping moment, she stared back at Roxy with an unreadable expression on her face.

"You will take good care now," she said, very softly, "won't you?"

Roxy's mouth was sandpaper. No words would have come out even if she'd tried. She nodded.

Mrs Smith nodded back, then turned and left the room. She closed the door quietly behind her.

"Oh my stars," Roxy whispered to the grit in her hand. "I don't believe it. We did it. *We did it!*"

The grit, because it was only a piece of grit – albeit a powerfully magic one – said nothing.

But now sleep was washing over Roxy anyway. She could do nothing but hope that when she woke up, she would remember it all…

**1**

**FOUR MONTHS LATER.**

It was towards the end of a chilly afternoon in early spring. The sun was just starting to set, and hundreds of people had formed a queue outside Snelling's department store on the Royal Boulevard in Rexopolis.

The grand store's glamorous façade, usually a gleaming white marble, had been shrouded in enormous silk drapes in a shade of deepest midnight blue. The only part of the storefront that had been left shroudless were the ornate gold revolving doors. Above the largest of these was a huge midnight-blue poster featuring six words:

# H-BOMB AND THE MISSILES: SWEET AGONY

This was the reason for the snaking queue, and for the atmosphere of barely controlled excitement in the chilly dusk air: H-Bomb and the Missiles, the biggest band in the entire world, had chosen to launch their latest album in their home city of Rexopolis. The band's legion of devoted fans were practically swooning with anticipation, mostly thanks to the rumour sweeping the queue like wildfire: that H-Bomb himself, the lead singer and the band's biggest star, was going to show up to the exclusive launch party, *right here in Snelling's tonight*.

Roxy Humperdinck, who was watching the queue from the other side of the Royal Boulevard, knew this would never happen. H-Bomb had not visited Rexopolis for over five years. He hadn't visited *anywhere* in Illustria, in fact. She had been exactly seven years old the last time he had come home, and even then it had only been a flying visit, under cover of darkness and surrounded by burly, sunglasses-wearing security guards, to catch the last ten minutes of her own, rather underwhelming seventh birthday party.

This was not because Roxy had won some meet-a-star contest, or anything of the sort. It was because H-Bomb – otherwise known as Han Humperdinck – was in fact her older half-brother. If he hadn't come home since – not even for any of the birthdays he shared with his twin sister, Gretel – there was *no way* he was going to be joining his bandmates in Snelling's music department today to sign autographs and pose for selfies. Anyway, Roxy wasn't here for autographs or selfies. She was here for another reason entirely.

She reached into her bag and took out The Letter.

She did not need to reread it. Thanks to her somewhat freaky (though admittedly useful) talent for remembering every word of everything she ever read, Roxy had already committed the entire letter to memory within three seconds of opening it yesterday morning.

And it wasn't as if it was exactly a long letter.

But it was certainly an extremely *strange* letter:

---

SEVENTH March

Dear Roxy,

I've now come to my decision that I yearn to feel feet in shoes. On the ground I do walk along a shiny floor there, not quickly, I can enjoy Snelling's perfumed smell and imagine a swanky store where very smart people will stroll tomorrow.

Your good and always loyal friend,

P.M.

---

There were several things about this letter that had raised Roxy's suspicions.

There was the fact that Roxy did not have, nor had she ever had, a friend with the initials PM.

There were the faint stains of (probably) ketchup and (possibly) mustard smeared across the rather crumpled paper, as if it had been absent-mindedly used as a napkin after a hot dog.

There was, unavoidably, the fact that not a single sentence in it made ANY SENSE WHATSOEVER.

But then, Roxy had quickly surmised, it wasn't really a "letter" at all, was it? It was a message, *in code*. So there really could be no doubt – no doubt at all – about who had sent it.

*Jones.*

While Roxy and Jones had been on their adventure together – when they had befriended Rumpelstiltskin, met the witch who had once cursed Sleeping Beauty, hijacked an enchanted flying minibus, discovered the location of the super-powerful Seventh Witching Stone (that kept Illustria filled with Decent Magic rather than Diabolical Magic) *and* turned Snow White's evil stepmother into a giant vegan muffin – one of the many useful things Jones had taught Roxy was the basics of code-cracking. (She had also taught Roxy a great number of extremely useless things, mostly to do with cupcakes, doughnuts and sausages.)

The old and extremely smelly book that Jones had been hunting for when she and Roxy had first met – *Mrs Tabitha Cattermole's Chronicle of the Cursed Kingdom* – had been written in a secret code. Reading only *every eleventh word* on one particular page had pieced together the information they had needed to locate the Seventh Stone: the most powerful of the seven magical stones that helped to maintain the False Memory Enchantment over not only Illustria but also the entire world. These stones could channel any enchantment, in fact – good or evil – which was why it had been so important that the Seventh Stone had not fallen into the hands of anyone with Diabolical intent.

Well: this mustard-tainted letter that Roxy was holding right now had a heavily scrawled **SEVENTH** at the top.

"*Come to ground floor,*" Roxy muttered to herself, picking out every SEVENTH word. "*Snelling's store …tomorrow p.m.*"

Of course, Roxy thought, it was possible that she had got it wrong; that perhaps she was only supposed to start reading every seventh word *after* the date.

In which case, the letter said: *My feet do not smell very good.*

No. No, no. It had to be the Snelling's thing.

Roxy took a deep breath, pulled on her headphones as if they were a security blanket, and headed towards the revolving door that wasn't designated for groupies.

*Wow*, was all she could think, as she stepped onto the shop floor. *Just … wow.*

She had never been into the posh store before, but now that she was here, she could see that Snelling's was a place of gleaming marble, of highly polished glass counters displaying expensive-looking luxuries, and of perfectly coiffed sales assistants. The ground floor was huge, stretching in a vast rectangle from the entrance doors all the way to gilt-painted escalators at the back and at each side. It seemed to be home to the Handbag department, the Lipstick department, an area dedicated solely to printed silk scarves, and a row of counters where a terrifying bevy of young women lined up like a kind of hairsprayed guard of honour to spritz you with unwanted perfume from cut-glass bottles. But most intimidatingly of all, there were *celebrities* everywhere: a famous TV presenter pushing past Roxy with an irritable huff … a girl band posing for selfies as they sailed up the escalator … and wasn't that smirking, way-too-tanned and way, way-too-toothy figure bellowing into his phone *Prince Ludovic* himself? Well, perhaps it was to be expected:

Snelling's was, after all, the place where all Illustria's top celebs did their shopping.

And Snelling's, Roxy decided, was also just about the scariest place she had ever been *in her life*. This included the time she had once fallen into a dungeon belonging to an unhinged witch who wanted to steal her hair and lock her away in a teetering tower for the rest of her life.

She pulled her hood up, put her head down and headed past the perfume counters towards the main escalator.

Which was when a sudden sharp jet of liquid was sprayed right into her face.

"Agggghhh!" Roxy clamped her hands to her smarting eyes and yanked off her headphones. "What on earth…!"

"My bad," a voice hissed back at her. "But don't make a scene, whatever you do!"

*"Jones?"*

"No! I'm not Jones! I'm Trudie Splashback, trainee scent consultant!"

But Roxy would have recognized Jones's voice anywhere. Opening her perfume-drenched eyelids one stinging centimetre, she could see, too, that it was Jones.

All right, it was a Jones quite unlike the Jones she

remembered from last year. This Jones was wearing bright-white overalls with an embroidered gold Snelling's logo, teetering black patent high heels that made her a good ten centimetres taller than her usual diminutive height, and a shiny but rather lopsided black bobbed wig. She wore thick make-up around her eyes and the glossy coral shade on her lips looked as if it had been applied with a garden shovel.

All the same, Jones it most certainly was.

"No, you're definitely…"

"Don't go and blow my blooming cover!" Jones glowered at Roxy from beneath the wonky wig, then reached up a hand to straighten it. "Honestly, didn't I teach you anything?"

"But what are you…? Why are you…? How are you…?"

"You're after some Nuit Royal, you say, madam?" Jones suddenly adopted a rather high-pitched, singsong voice quite unlike her own, as a sharp-faced manager glanced over at them from the nearest counter. "The massive one-litre bottle of our brand-new exclusive commemorative H-Bomb and the Missiles scent?"

"I … er…"

"I don't think I've got that particular size behind the counter, madam, but if you'd like to pop along with me while I check the storeroom, I'm sure we'll be able to find it! We'll have you smelling exactly like a famously reclusive rock star in no time at all."

Before Roxy could reply, Jones had grasped her by the elbow and was steering her through the crowds towards the escalator.

"Just keep smiling," she muttered, out of one side of her glossy mouth. "Don't raise any suspicions."

"But aren't *you* raising suspicions?" Roxy hissed back. "Pretending to be a perfume salesgirl?"

"I *am* a perfume salesgirl! Have been for a whole week!"

"But you're not old enough to get a job!"

"Hence the disguise!" said Jones, gesturing towards her outfit, from her high-heeled shoes all the way up to her bobbed wig. "Pretty good, right?"

"Not really, no! You still look like a very small twelve-year old …"

"I'm thirteen now, *actually*!"

"… wearing a bad wig and too much make-up and a pair of shoes you can hardly walk in."

"Hey, I can walk in these!" hissed Jones, stumbling onto the first step of the escalator, then doing a little dance from foot to foot while grimacing in pain. "OK, OK, I admit it, the shoes suck," she went on. "But if they help convince my boss I'm really Trudie

20

Splashback, sixteen years old and eager for a job selling H-Bomb perfume – that smells, by the way, *exactly* like my great-grandad's least-hygienic tea towel – then they're worth all the blisters and the chafing and the burning pain on my soles that *literally never lets up.*

"Why are you looking so furtive?" she suddenly demanded, as Roxy pulled her hood closer about her face. "You're perfectly entitled to be in this store, you know. I mean, sure, you don't look like your typical Snelling's customer, but nobody can actually throw you out for that. There are all kinds of people here today for the album launch. Oooooh, I meant to ask, actually – do *you* think H-Bomb is going to show up to the VIP party? I've got a bet with one of the other perfume-spray girls that he won't, but she's sure he will. I just thought you might have the inside track, seeing as he's your brother and everything—"

"How would I know what my brother is or isn't going to do?" Roxy replied, sharply. "Anyway, shouldn't we be talking about how you didn't contact me for months – thanks for that, by the way; it felt great to be totally abandoned – and then, all of a sudden, you send this letter..."

"Did you like my code? It was a good one, wasn't it? I got it from good old Mrs Tabitha!" Jones pulled Roxy off the smoothly purring escalator at the second floor and onto the one that led up to the third. "Anyway, I may not have actually been in touch, but that doesn't mean I haven't been keeping an eye on you."

"You mean *spying*?"

"Define *spying*."

"Watching me. Following me. Tracking my movements."

"Oh, right, then yes, I've been spying on you. But not in a *bad* way." Jones wafted a dismissive hand. "I just needed to be sure that before I contacted you, you weren't being watched, or anything."

"By somebody other than you, you mean," Roxy pointed out.

"Well, better to have *me* spying on you than anybody from the Ministry. And I can now safely say, Roxy, that there is nobody from the Ministry spying on you. Which means you must have done a pretty awesome job of convincing them that they successfully wiped your memory and re-enchanted you." Jones lowered her voice to a bare whisper and glanced over her shoulder as they changed escalators again. "I'm thinking that tiny piece of Witching Stone must have worked, right?"

Without even thinking, Roxy moved her hand to the pocket of her hoodie, to clasp her fingers around the tiny piece of Witching Stone. She did this a lot these days. She could not explain why, but her hand just felt *better* with the little nub of grit inside it. "Yes. It worked. I used it with the magic-blocking spell Frankie taught me."

"Woah." Beneath the thick mascara, Jones's cornflower-blue eyes were saucers. "Frankie's spell – I'm impressed. Let's face it, that could have gone badly wrong."

Frankie, Jones's fairy godmother, was a three-hundred-and-sixty-four-year-old lady fairy who – thanks to a poorly executed makeover spell just before Roxy first met her – had accidentally taken on the appearance of a ten-year-old boy. Still, Frankie's magic-blocking spell had managed to prevent Mrs Smith's False Memory Enchantment from taking hold of Roxy back in the Decontamination Zone all those months ago, leaving Roxy able to remember absolutely everything that had happened on her adventure with Jones. So Frankie's magic couldn't be *completely* useless.

"Which reminds me," Jones went on. "Talking of magic, how are you getting on with that online spell provider I signed you up for?"

"I knew it!" Roxy let go of the Witching Stone grit and pulled out her phone. "I knew it was you! Who else would have signed me up for a so-called free trial of *Dodgy Magic A-Go-Go*?"

"It's not called *Dodgy Magic A-Go-Go*, and you know it," retorted Jones. "It's called *Basic Incantations at Thy Fingertips*, and I went to a lot of trouble to find it, I'll have you know. It's not easy locating genuine magic providers in a country that likes to pretend magic doesn't exist! I spent hours hunting on the internet for something suitable! I don't know what would have happened if my stepmum had walked in and caught me on her laptop when I was meant to be polishing her underpants, or whatever thankless chores she had dumped on me."

"But what on earth do we need basic incantations for?" Roxy asked, knowing too well by now that there was no point expressing sympathy about Jones's horrible stepmother. Jones did not take kindly to anyone – even Roxy – taking an interest in her terrible home life. "I mean, whatever this thing is you're *onto*, how are some slightly rubbish spells for opening stuck jam-jar lids or getting your shopping bags to fly home from the supermarket supposed to help? Because those are the only spells they've sent me so far, you know. And now they're trying to charge me for new ones!"

"Yeah, sorry about that. I'd have got the app myself, but you know I don't have a phone. Besides,

I thought you'd *like* to be given special responsibility for magic, after that amazing stunt you pulled turning Queen Bellissima into a vegan muffin! You're the one who knows how to work that bit of grit, after all. And we're going to need all the special skills we can muster on this mission, Roxy." Jones lowered her voice, dramatically, as they stepped onto their final escalator. "Something *huge* is going on."

"Going on *here*," Roxy asked, dubiously, "at Snelling's department store? Something apart from this album launch and snooty party, that is?"

"No, not something going on at Snelling's, exactly! It's more … well, that it *started* here. We're getting off now," Jones added, pulling Roxy off the escalator as it reached the fifth floor. "This way."

"*Outward Bound department*," Roxy read aloud from the sign at the top of the escalator. "What's that?"

"Mountaineering equipment, rucksacks … all that cool sort of stuff. And best of all –" Jones was leading the way across the much-quieter fifth floor towards a far corner, well away from even the one or two customers browsing fleece gilets and bobble hats – "*tents*!" she finished, with immense satisfaction.

"They're very nice tents, Jones," Roxy said, looking at the admittedly impressive array of tents spread out in this corner. "But I don't quite see—"

"Come on in!" Jones interrupted. She crouched down, wobbling on her high heels, and pulled aside the canvas door of a bright-orange tent right at the front of the display.

"Jones!" Roxy hissed, ducking down beside her before anyone saw them. "We can't just go into one of these without permission!"

"I don't need permission." Jones cast a wide grin over her shoulder before disappearing inside. "I live here."

"You *what*?" Roxy asked, following.

"I. Live. Here." Jones swept a hand round the tiny tent's interior. "Home sweet home. Or tent sweet tent, I suppose. If you're going to nitpick."

"Jones, you … you can't *live* here. I mean, even if you've run away from home again…"

"Hey. Living with my stepmum and stepsisters isn't *home*." Jones's lips set like stone. "Got it?"

"Sorry. But Jones … this is just a tent. In a department store. I mean, I don't even see a sleeping bag, or a stove to heat up so much as a tin of beans…"

"Oh, Roxy, Roxy, Roxy," Jones sighed. "What *are* we going to do about that limited imagination of yours?" She turned towards the back of the cramped tent, lifted one corner of the canvas, and – surprisingly – began to crawl out of it. She glanced back over one shoulder, her eyes glittering. "So, are you coming with me or not?"

## 2

Roxy was startled to realize, as she exited the tent behind Jones, that she was not emerging back out into the tent display. Rather, she was exiting into a short tunnel that appeared to have been ingeniously fashioned from… She stopped and reached up a hand to feel.

"Jones, are these *duvet covers*?"

"Yep! Seventh floor – Bedlinen & Homewares. They're king-size duvet covers draped over trellises. Which are from the fourth floor – Gardens & Patios."

"You've raided the entire store," Roxy said, rather faintly.

"Not the *entire* store! I still haven't found any use for the eighth floor – Pianos & Harpsichords. But never say never! (You never know when you might need a harpsichord in a hurry, right?)"

"Uh…"

"Anyway, it's amazing what you can find when you get to sneak around Snelling's after dark! I know it looks like it's just a store for stuck-up poshos and celebrities, but I'll be honest with you, Roxy, those stuck-up poshos and celebrities sure do have some awesome stuff to spend their money on!" Jones had reached the end of the tunnel and was lifting up a canvas flap to what looked like another tent. "Prepare to have your mind one hundred and fifty per cent *blown*!"

It was not, exactly, another tent.

It was maybe nine or ten – or eleven, or twelve? – tents *all connected together*. There was an absolute warren of them: half a dozen linked tents formed a massive square in the centre, and several more led off in actual corridors and alleyways to the left and right.

"Welcome," declaimed Jones, in the sort of booming voice they use in movie trailers, "to *Tent City*."

"It's… I just… Jones, have you *shoplifted* all this stuff?" croaked Roxy.

Because the tents were not empty. Far from it. Jones had obviously raided several other departments after dark – Bedroom Furniture, Toys & Games and Kitchen Equipment, at a minimum. In one corner of the first tent was a single wooden bed decorated with a range of giant cuddly toys, from a colossal bear to a rather disturbingly proportioned cat with the word *Snelling's* stamped on a yellow ribbon around its neck. In the opposite corner there was a snazzy little kitchen area, complete with a top-of-the-range microwave, mini-fridge, sandwich toaster, and – in pride of place – a gleaming silver coffee machine. To the right of *this* was a sitting area: beanbags, a rather nice leather armchair and a low coffee table with stack after stack of papers piled perilously high between used tin mugs, bowls encrusted with what looked like gravy, and several packets of half-eaten sweets.

"Hey, nothing's been *shoplifted*!" said Jones, defensively. "I mean, it only counts as *shoplifting* if you *lift* it out of the *shop*, right? And if you don't plan to give it back. But I have every intention of giving it back, and in pristine condition, too! Well, OK, the sandwich toaster might be a bit worse for wear, but that's only because I've discovered this amazing way of toasting sausage sandwiches. See, what you do is, you get yourself some of these awesome sausages from the lower ground floor – Gourmet Foods & Luxury Groceries – and then you need some nice soft bread, and plenty of mustard, and—"

"OK, enough about sausage sandwiches!" Roxy folded her arms and glared at Jones. "You're going to explain this whole thing to me right now, or I'm leaving this tent …"

"Tent *City*," said Jones, piously, "*please*."

"… and I'm walking away, and I'm not coming back. And I know you need me for this new mission, Jones, because you've already said so! I'm the one with the 'freaky photographic memory', remember. And I'm the one who knows how to work the Witching Stone fragment. And thanks to you, I'm even the one with these stupid spells on my phone! So either you tell me everything –" she took a step towards the duvet-cover tunnel – "or it's goodbye from Roxy!"

At least Jones had the decency to look a little bit impressed by this speech. "OK, OK. I tell you what – why don't you take a seat instead of flouncing about pretending you're going to walk away, and I'll show you something?" She was already kneeling beside the coffee table, rifling through the piles of papers. "Coffee machine instruction manual," she muttered. "Voucher for ten per cent off in Snelling's Eyebrow Bar… Hmm, do you reckon that means they only tweeze ninety per cent of the hairs out of your eyebrows, or— Oooooh, mini marshmallows!" she exclaimed, as one of the open bags of sweets tipped over slightly, sending a handful of pink and white marshmallows sprawling over the paperwork. "Ha!"

she added, a moment later, through a mouthful. "This is what I was looking for!" She swiped a single piece of paper off the pile and gripped it tightly. "Have you ever heard," she asked, in a low, urgent voice, "of the Missing?"

"The missing what?"

"*The* Missing," whispered Jones.

Roxy blinked at her.

"Of course." Jones nodded, infuriatingly pompous. "I forget, sometimes, how little you know about the Cursed Kingdom."

"Hey, I know plenty! I know the Cursed Kingdom was the old name for Illustria, until the Great Clean-Up twenty-one years ago. I know that in those days, evil magic ruled over everyone who lived here. I know that there were Decent-Magical folk, too, and I know that they're still living in Illustria today!"

This had been one of the most mind-blowing things she had learned from Jones: that so-called BOBIs – magical Beings of Benign Intent – still lived amongst ordinary people in Illustria. Frankie, Jones's fairy godmother, was just one of many BOBIs living secretly amongst non-magical folk, although no BOBI was allowed to practise their magic without a strict licence, issued by the top-secret Ministry Overseeing, Organizing Or Occasionally Opposing Hocus-Pocus.

In fact MOOOOOH was so incredibly secret that it pretended, instead, to be the Ministry for Soup. This was where Roxy's much older half-sister Gretel worked, pretending to be a cleaner when, in fact, she was a kick-butt secret agent. It was only this fake identity, which Gretel had hidden from her own sister for years, that eased Roxy's conscience a little about pretending to have had her memory wiped by Mrs Smith. But not that much better. She still felt queasy every time she dwelt on it for too long.

"You've got that look on your face again," Jones observed, "by the way."

"What look?"

"That look that says you're stressing about what your sister would say if she knew about any of this. If she knew you'd managed to evade being re-enchanted. If she knew you were here in Snelling's, meeting a fugitive from justice…"

"You're not a fugitive from justice!" Roxy snapped. "Nobody at the Ministry even knows you exist, thanks to me covering for you!

"Fair point," Jones said generously. "But we don't have time for you to be a massive stress-bucket. We have a mission to complete. Allow me to present you –" she handed the piece of paper to Roxy – "with our very first clue."

"We have a *clue*? Oh, no." Roxy stared at Jones. "This isn't something you've decoded from the pages of Mrs Tabitha Cattermole again, is it?"

"Nope. It's a newspaper article. From several years ago." Jones's voice had become deliberately casual. "An article which, it just so happens, was written by my father."

"I didn't know your dad was a journalist!" Roxy exclaimed. "I thought he was—" She stopped herself, just in time, from saying that from the little Jones had told her about her father (who was now dead), she had assumed he had been a slightly unhinged conspiracy theorist.

"Yes, he was a journalist!" Jones glared at her. "Why else do you think he was always asking so many questions about the suspicious ways things work in Illustria? Did you take him for some kind of unhinged conspiracy theorist, or something?"

Roxy busied herself staring at the piece of paper, which seemed to be a cutting from a newspaper. She was too bad a liar to risk replying.

"Anyway," Jones went on, "I found this article stuffed right at the bottom of a box of his things in the attic a couple of weeks ago. My stupid stepsisters made me go up there to find some stupid dressing-up box for a stupid costume party they were hosting. Oh, and that copy is the only evidence this article ever existed, by the way," Jones added, her eyes glittering meaningfully. "You can't find it anywhere on the Internet. Not even so much as a dead link. Tell me that's not suspicious!"

Roxy sat down in a buttery-soft armchair and started to read.

## INCIDENT AT SNELLING'S ROOF GARDEN: "UNFORTUNATE BUT NOT AT ALL IMPORTANT," SAY MINISTRY OFFICIALS
### By Jimmy Jones

Revellers enjoying a night out at the Snelling's famous rooftop nightclub in downtown Rexopolis were interrupted yesterday by a violent disturbance. Partygoers reported the sudden appearance of an "extremely distressed woman, seemingly out of nowhere," according to one. The woman proceeded to "howl like a deranged wolf" at terrified clubbers, and smashed several cocktail glasses "in a frenzy". Several Roof Garden security staff attempted unsuccessfully to subdue the woman before police were called. As she was taken away in an auxiliary SMOG vehicle, passers-by described how the woman began shouting, "Go on, then, tell them about Sky Zone!" and "Why doesn't anybody care about the missing?"

The woman, who was briefly detained before being allowed to return home, has been identified as Ms Susan-Bedelia Little, 36, an engineer working for the Soup Ministry. Senior Ministry spokesperson Mrs Smith gave the following statement: *"One of our highly valued scientists, Ms Susan-Bedelia Little, has found that the stresses of a government job have simply become too much for her. After this most unfortunate – but thankfully really, really unimportant – incident at Snelling's Roof Garden, Little has decided to leave her post with immediate effect. We all very much hope that she will take this opportunity for what is clearly some much-needed rest and recuperation."*

Snelling's owner, Sandford S. Snelling Jr, said: "We apologize unreservedly for this unexpected incident. All the guests that were enjoying our hospitality at the time – personally tailored cocktails, sixty-two different varieties of champagne and a selection of exquisite nibbles from around the world – have naturally been given a full refund. Snelling's Roof Garden remains open for business, and we look forward to welcoming many more of our cherished guests in the future."

"Mrs Smith!" exclaimed Roxy.

"*A selection of exquisite nibbles from around the world!*" Jones said. "But yeah," she added, hastily, "let's focus on the important stuff. If Mrs Smith popping up like a bad penny in this incident isn't proof of a massive Ministry cover-up, I don't know what is."

"But what were they covering up?" Roxy felt as if things were getting muddier, whereas Jones seemed to be experiencing crystal clarity. "What's any of this stuff from seven years ago got to do with this *missing* thing, anyway? And who do you think this –" she glanced down at the article – "Susan-Bedelia Little is?"

"That's where it gets even dodgier!" Jones hooted. "I can't find her *anywhere*! She doesn't have a SelfSpace page. There's no Twaddle account in her name – and it's a seriously odd name, so she'd stand out like a sore thumb if she was on there."

"So *she's* the thing that's missing?"

"No, no. She *is* missing. But she's not *the* Missing—" Jones was interrupted by a sudden bleep from the watch she was wearing. (A rather snazzy-looking watch, Roxy couldn't help thinking, which looked exactly as if it had been not-strictly shoplifted from the second floor – Watches & Fine Jewellery.) "Oh. My. Stars! It's six o'clock! We have to hurry!"

"We have to be somewhere?"

"We certainly do!" Jones was already pulling off her bobbed wig to reveal her real hair – currently dyed bright tangerine – and starting to remove the high-heeled shoes. "We've got to get to this party! Don't worry," she added, before Roxy could utter the words, *Wait – party? What party?* "I've already picked you out a fabulous outfit! Just pop through there –" she gestured towards one of the tent corridors – "and you'll find it folded on top of the harpsichord."

"*Harpsichord*, Jones?"

"Oh. Yeah. I kind of lied when I said I hadn't found any use for the eighth floor. But come on – what better opportunity to finally learn to play one? And it only took me four hours to wheel it to the service lift and out again. Now hurry, hurry!" Jones flapped her hands at Roxy. "We'll never find the answers to our mystery if we don't get to that party."

"You don't mean … the VIP H-Bomb album launch party?"

"What other party would I mean?"

"But what on earth will we find there?" Roxy was baffled. "A bunch of minor celebrities – who aren't even proper H-Bomb fans, by the way – posing for selfies?"

"Oh, I'll tell you what we're going to find." Jones

was taking a second piece of paper off the coffee table. She handed it to Roxy. "Read this," she breathed. "It's a letter Susan Whoosit Little once wrote to my dad."

The paper was wrinkled and wafery. "Did you find this in the attic too?" Roxy asked.

Jones nodded. "Once you've read it, you'll understand why we have to get up to the Roof Garden. We're going to find the secret entrance to SkyZone."

Dear Mr Jones,

First. I want to thank you very much indeed for your kind letter of 21st July.

Second. I cannot tell you how much I appreciated your words. No lie to say they brought a tear to my eye. Has any stranger ever been more thoughtful?

Third. How much longer do you think we will enjoy the fine weather we've been having? And what about this lovely warmth? Really, it's the nicest we've had in ages. I'm not missing the rain.

Fourth. If perhaps you will permit me to say, I admire your writing very much. Really, Mr Jones, you are talented. If we might meet one day, I will shower you with compliments! Some people tell me I should write, but I have no skill at it. I hit the roof if I have to write more than a few sentences.

Fifth. Sitting in my small garden, I like to watch the birds. Several have now arrived at once. I really must visit Snelling's and buy a new bird table. On Wednesday, perhaps, shall I go. Maybe then sweet robins will come. These birds perform a show for me. I know many — including you, I'm sure — think that's absurd. But they make no secret of the fun they're having. Making their dramatic little entrance and exit! Really these birds come to eat the seed I leave for them. Then off into the sky again. If I can, I zone out their chirping.

With warmest wishes,

Susan

## 3

"Jeez, Louise, Roxy!" snapped Jones, fifteen minutes later. "Will you just stop *scratching*?"

They had stepped off on the seventeenth floor (Gifts), which was as high as it was possible to go by escalator – the Roof Garden nightclub itself had to be reached by a door across the other side of the shop floor – and were making their way through displays of overpriced bath bombs and twee little photo frames with kittens on them.

"I can't help it!" Roxy gazed down, despairingly, at the frock she was now wearing. This was the party outfit Jones had picked out for her, and it was vomit-inducing: an ankle-length powder-blue satin ballgown with tidal waves of frothy lace all around the sleeves and the neckline. There was a matching satin shoulder bag that Jones had insisted she carry – "Because look, it's got a teeny-tiny inner pocket where you can slot the Witching Stone fragment! WAY safer than the pocket of that blooming hoodie you're always wearing!" – and for some inexplicable reason there was also a pair of matching shoes: buckled Mary Janes in the same blue satin, with a low heel that made Roxy feel even more abnormally tall than usual. "How come *you* get to wear something simple, and actually quite nice?" she hissed.

Jones was wearing a cocktail frock of her own, which, unlike Roxy's frilled horror, was simple and elegant: plain black silk, and without a flounce or an itchy bit of lace in sight. It did not quite match the battered brown leather kitbag she took everywhere, nor the old brown boots she had declared she couldn't possibly do without, but in typical Jones style she was pulling the whole look off with, well, style. Even the black wig she had put on over her tangerine-coloured hair was working. She looked beautiful, and cool, and totally ready to rock this party, whereas Roxy felt none of these things.

"Hey, this was the only thing in Ladies' Formal Wear that fitted me," Jones said, unconvincingly.

"Really? Because I think you chose something you actually liked, while I'm stuck in this awful, sweaty scratch-fest, looking like I'm wearing a paper doily…"

"Look, we've got bigger things to focus on than the fact that, yes, OK, you do totally look like you're wearing a paper doily," declared Jones. "Now, we're agreed on the meaning of Susan Little's code, right? We're obviously meant to read the first word of every sentence in the first paragraph, and the second word of every sentence in the second paragraph, and so on." She reached into her backpack, not even breaking step to do so, and pulled out the letter Roxy had read back at Tent City. *"I … cannot … lie … any … longer … about … the … missing … will … you … meet … me … roof … garden … at … Snelling's … I … will … show … you … secret … entrance … to … Sky … Zone.* Right?"

"Right," Roxy agreed. "Though we've still no idea what SkyZone actually is."

"Speak for yourself!" snorted Jones.

"You mean, you *know*?"

"Oh, I have a fair few theories," said Jones, airily. "You don't get to be an expert on the history of the Cursed Kingdom without working out a thing or two."

"So, any of these super-brilliant theories you'd care to share with me," Roxy asked, rolling her eyes, "or…"

"I recognize that gentle voice!" came a voice from the middle of a display wall at the far end. "Dear Roxy, is it you?"

Roxy stared over at the display wall. It was cluttered

with wall clocks with ghastly artificial cuckoos, a pink-painted wooden sign that said *Live Simply, Laugh Often, Love with No Regrets*, and a selection of shabby-chic vintage-style mirrors, one of which was a s*midge* shabbier and less chic than all the others...

"*Mirror?*" gasped Roxy.

"Why yes, it's me!" shrieked the mirror. Not only was it shabby – with a tarnished frame and slightly smudged glass – but it also had an air of MASSIVE OUTRAGE. The air-of-massive-outrage thing was not a surprise to Roxy, though – nor the fact that the mirror appeared to be talking – because this was their old friend Mirror, an enchanted talking mirror they'd met in the tower of the hair-obsessed witch. He spoke in rhyme because this was the way all magical objects spoke, a fact that was rather charming until you had to put up with hours and hours of it. "Oh, get me down! I need a cuddle, too!"

"Of course, Mirror, you poor thing!" Roxy hurried to the display and took Mirror down off the wall, glad there was nobody around, so close to closing time, to see her hugging a looking glass. "What on earth are you doing here?"

"Yeah, what on earth *are* you doing here?" demanded Joncs, folding her arms and eyeballing Mirror. "I left you on the third floor – Luxury Home Interiors!"

"*You left Mirror? All alone in Snelling's?*" Roxy turned on her friend. "Jones, you were meant to keep it at your stepmum's! So you'd have someone there who *cared about you*! How could you just *abandon* it like this?"

"Hey, I didn't *abandon* it! I said I'd go back and visit every few days. Admittedly, I kind of forgot about that part. But even if I *had* remembered," Jones went on, "I wouldn't have found it, would I? Thanks to someone moving it all the way up here to the Pointless Tat department…"

"Not Pointless Tat!" howled Mirror. "You ghastly girl! It's *Gifts*, as well you know! Though I am *not* a gift, of course, but couldn't tell them so."

"Well, of course you're not a gift, Mirror!" Roxy soothed. "Perhaps you were just too … uh … too *unique* for the Luxury Home Interiors department."

"Yes, Roxy, dear, I think that's right," agreed Mirror, before snapping in Jones's direction again, "but *she's* not one to care! The very day we came to town, she left me hanging there."

"Yeah, because you *never stopped talking*!" retorted Jones. "It was a massive security risk while we were living at my stepmother's, and an even more massive security risk here at Snelling's! Not to mention," she went on, in a much lower voice, to Roxy, "I literally couldn't handle it myself. I mean, while we were at my stepmum's, I deliberately put it on the wall in front of the TV so it wouldn't *keep on trying to chat*, but then it discovered quiz shows…" She rolled her eyes. "And if there's one thing worse than an enchanted object wittering at you every minute of the day, it's an enchanted object asking if you know the capital of Cambodia or which herb is used to flavour a béarnaise sauce."

"I only seek to pass the time!" shrieked Mirror. "To have a friendly chat! But fine – I shall not speak at all! Let's see how you like *that*!"

"I'd be absolutely fine with it, actually, Mirror," said Jones, glancing up at the cuckoo clocks on the wall. "And seriously, we don't have time to stand around – we need to get up to that party before they close the doors. Bring Mirror if you want, Roxy," she added, already setting out across the shop floor again, "but you'll have to hide it under all those layers of horrible, scratchy lace. We need to go under the radar at this party."

"I k*new* you thought this dress was scratchy and horrible!" said Roxy, feeling almost as outraged as Mirror. Tucking Mirror tightly under one frothy armpit, she hurried after Jones. "Anyway, how come we have to go to this party at all? Haven't you had any other chances to get into the nightclub since you've been living here? You've managed to creep around the rest of the store!"

"Nope." Jones shook her head, making her tangerine hair bounce from side to side. "The nightclub hasn't been open since I've been working here – they've been refurbishing it, you know, especially for this posh launch party – and the doors are always locked during the day. Anyway, it's pretty handy that we get to gatecrash a party while we're checking out the Roof Garden. I mean, where better to stock up on fabulous free snacks to take on our mission?"

"Wait – did you say *gatecrash*?" Roxy hissed, anxiously, as they approached a set of rather shiny glass doors at the rear of the seventeenth floor, where – oh, *no* – there stood an extremely large security man and a young woman with severe hair and a large clipboard. "But how will we get past *them*?"

"Oh, Roxy. Don't you think I've thought of that?" Jones was already reaching into her backpack and pulling out the very bottle of Nuit Royal she'd assaulted Roxy with a couple of hours earlier. "Just go along with everything I say," she hissed.

Roxy's heart sank into her satin buckled shoes as she dutifully trailed Jones up to the glass door.

"Good evening," purred Jones. "My name is Trudie Splashback, trainee scent consultant, and I've just been allocated the job of tonight's official perfume dispenser." She held up the cut-glass bottle and posed, prettily. "Would either of you care to try our exclusive H-Bomb commemorative scent? It's unisex."

"Commemorative scent?" The young woman with the clipboard didn't even bother to meet Jones's eye. "I don't *think* so. Run along, now."

"I most certainly will *not* run along!" Jones snapped, before remembering that she was supposed to be Trudie Splashback, and putting on the singsong voice again. "We received an urgent call in the perfume hall just before closing time to let us know that there are *top celebrities* at this party who forgot to put on any perfume before they came out. I don't think I need to tell you what a recipe for disaster *that* could turn out to be."

"Are you implying," asked the young woman, finally deigning to glance down at Jones, "that the VIPs at this party are *smelly*?"

"Well, think about it – a sweaty dancefloor, hot lights, the steam from what I'm pretty sure are some seriously delicious sausage-based canapés…" Jones ticked the list off on her fingers. "I'm sure you understand what a heady mixture that could prove to be!"

The colossal security man towered over Roxy and Jones.

"Tell you what, love," he said, in a steady but menacing tone. "You can take your exclusive scent—"

"Awesome, thanks!" Jones took a step in the direction of the glass doors, only to have her way barred by his immense little finger.

"… and you can shove off," he finished. "Right?" he added, turning to look at the young woman with the clipboard.

"Oh, *absolutely*," began the woman, just as the glass doors opened behind her and a head poked out, wearing dark shades.

Roxy stifled a gasp. It was a head she recognized.

It belonged to Solomon Sax, the drummer in H-Bomb and the Missiles.

So at least *one* of the band had come to the launch party! It made sense, thought Roxy, that out of the five members, Sax would be the one who showed up. H-Bomb might be the lead singer and the one the fans worshipped, but Sax was the one who really lived the rock-star life: he partied, he jet-setted, and barely a week went by that did not see the gossip magazine filled with paparazzi shots of him strutting out of swanky restaurants or beachside bars.

"You're in charge of security, right? Because I thought I'd made it absolutely clear," drawled Solomon Sax, in his transatlantic twang, "that I said I didn't wanna see any phones at this party?"

"You – you did, Mr Sax," stammered Clipboard Woman. "Has there been an incident?"

"Incident? There have been *incidents*," snapped Solomon Sax. More of him emerged from behind the glass doors; he was wearing a bright-red velvet suit and a shockingly purple shirt that was iced with SO MUCH FLOUNCY LACE that Roxy would have felt immediately better about her own appalling doily of a dress if she hadn't been trying, right at that moment, to hide behind Jones's backpack so that Sax didn't see her. "I'm tryna relax in there, just tryna chill out in that so-called chill-out zone, and every five seconds there's some random *fan* –" the drummer's upper lip curled, and he ran an elegant musician's hand through his long, dyed-black hair – "coming up to ask for a selfie— Hey. Wait a minute." He stopped, and pointed a long finger at Roxy. "You. I know you."

"Um … yes," Roxy shuffled out from behind the backpack, recognizing defeat. "Yes, you might do…"

"You're Han's baby sister." Solomon Sax smiled, a dazzling white smile. It was impossible to tell whether or not the smile reached his shaded eyes. He tapped his foot thoughtfully. "He has your picture on his phone."

"That's right – she's H-Bomb's sister!" Jones shoved

her arm through Roxy's and marched towards the doors. "That's why we have to be at this party. She hasn't even *seen* her brother in ... how many years is it now, Roxy?"

"Five," gulped Roxy, "but..."

"And I'm betting H-Bomb is here already, right?" Jones went on, sounding just as smoothly certain of this fact as she had sounded dismissive about it back in Tent City.

"Sure," said Solomon Sax, with a bored shrug. "He's here."

Han – *here*? Roxy felt her heart tighten. Here, at this nightclub ... in Rexopolis ... *in Illustria* ... after all the years he'd stayed away? Without telling her or Gretel that he was coming?

"Hey, I thought you were trying to claim you needed to be let in because you were some kind of pong-zapper," the security man was saying, only to be silenced by an elbow from Clipboard Woman.

"Of course you can go in, ladies!" she gushed, all smiles now as she ushered Roxy and Jones through the glass doors. "There's delicious food, fabulous drinks, a stunning chill-out area where you can relax on Bali beds and enjoy free foot massages from our roving reflexologists..."

Jones gave her a little wave as she swanned past.

"Oh, this is *properly* awesome," she said, breathlessly, as the doors slid shut behind them.

Even Roxy, still reeling at the news about her brother, was dimly aware that Jones had a point. The nightclub they had just entered was, by any standards, properly awesome. For starters, it looked – even seventeen floors up here on Snelling's rooftop – like a wild, exotic garden. It had a glass roof and glass walls that let in all the glowing orange light from the slowly setting sun. In the centre was a COLOSSAL central plant-stalk, as thick as a tree trunk, stretching all the way up to the high glass ceiling; myriad vivid green shoots, of all sizes, spiralled out of this stalk and crept in every direction. The club was *packed*: at least two hundred people were crammed in between the jungle of vines. The girl band from the escalator was doing some pretty cheesy dancing, in formation, over by the impressive sound system. Prince Ludovic bopped, in the centre of the dance-floor, with several very shiny-looking TV actresses. There were half a dozen *extremely* famous musicians sprawling, guitars in hand, on those low, chill-out Bali beds that Clipboard Woman had mentioned, arranged in a loose circle around the massive central stalk. Roxy could see the Missiles' bass player and lead guitarist amongst them. Of Han, though, there was no sign at all.

"Where is he?" she murmured, gazing around the throng.

"Told you he'd be here!" said Jones, cheerfully.

"No, you didn't! You placed a bet with your friend from the perfume hall that he *wouldn't*."

"Oh, yeah. I forgot you have that freakishly good memory," Jones sounded annoyed. "But look, it's good news! *You're* here, *he's* here … maybe you two can hang out!" She seemed to rethink this largesse almost immediately. "I mean, obviously we don't have a lot of spare time tonight – 'cos of being on a mission, and all that – but we might be able to spare, I dunno, five minutes, or something, while I stock up on nibbles for the journey. That bossy woman on the door said there was food, right?"

"I don't know if I even want to find him, Jones," Roxy said, miserably. "If he didn't think it was worth telling us he was coming to town…"

"OK, enough already about your family." Jones's wafer-thin patience had reached its limit. "Can we get back to my stuff now, please? Secret entrance? SkyZone? Remember?"

Roxy opened her mouth to tell Jones that actually, she would appreciate a little more sensitivity when she realized that actually, she wouldn't. Sensitivity was not what anyone needed Jones for. You needed

Jones for hidden entrances, and secret codes, and rampant shoplifting – all of which, right now, felt like they might be a very welcome distraction from the real problems in Roxy's world. "Secret entrance. Right. Where do you think we should start?"

"Well, first we should try to blend in," said Jones. "Can't you try to look a bit more relaxed, Roxy? Like you've been to a party in an exclusive nightclub before?"

"Jones, it may have escaped your notice," Roxy said, patiently, "but I'm thirteen. I've never been to a party in a nightclub before." She thought for a moment. "Actually, come to think of it, I've never been to a party *anywhere*."

"You've *never been to a party*?" Jones stared at her. "How is that even possible?"

"I've told you before: we moved house every time my dad married somebody new! I had a fresh town with each fresh stepmother," Roxy said, defensively. "You know you're the first real friend I've ever had."

"Then just try and *pretend* you've been to parties before. I mean, they're not exactly complicated. You're a music fan, aren't you? You can enjoy the music, for starters."

"Well, that's impossible," Roxy began. "It's Spencer Spark-Plugge. Rubbish synthetic pop. I bet Han is hating every beat, wherever he is…"

"And may I say, it's FAR TOO LOUD," came a bad-tempered voice from under Roxy's armpit. "My ears are simply ringing!"

"You don't have ears, Mirror," said Jones. "And anyway, I thought you were staying silent?"

"I only wish to comment," snapped Mirror, "on this dreadful tuneless singing!"

"It's OK, Mirror, I hate it too." Roxy took Mirror out from under her arm. "Are you OK? Is there anything you need?"

"Well, now you come to mention it …" began Mirror.

"Put it back!" hissed Jones. "Do you want to completely blow our cover?"

"… I'd love a little peek! A party! Wow! Though, Roxy, dear—"

"I mean it!" Jones grabbed Mirror from Roxy's hands and unzipped her kitbag. "It's going in here."

"YOU HAVE TO LET ME SPEAK!" yowled Mirror. "I know you think I'm just a bore, a lump of glass and metal! But I have seen what you have not! Behind you, guys – it's GRETEL!"

**4**

Roxy thought faster than she had ever thought in her entire life.

Those Bali beds forming a chill-out zone around the huge stalk: one of them was empty, and there was just about space to hide beneath its low frame.

She grabbed Jones and pulled them both under it.

And not a moment too soon, because before Jones could open her mouth to object, a pair of rubber clogs appeared in view at the end of the bed. They were elephant-dung grey, and battered, and *exactly* the same clogs that Roxy watched Gretel put on every morning, along with matching elephant-dung-grey overalls, to go to work in her massively fake job as a loo cleaner at the Soup Ministry.

"It's Gretel!" she mouthed at Jones, who was still bundling a squawking Mirror into her kitbag for safety

– and silence. "Mirror was right!"

The clogs had stopped, only an arm's length from Roxy and Jones. They were not moving.

"Why's she here?" Roxy whispered at Jones.

"Come on, kiddo." Jones shifted, trying to get comfortable in the narrow crawl space under the bed. "You know why."

"What do you mean?"

"You really don't know?"

"No!"

"She must have come here to meet your brother!" Jones hissed.

*But … that would mean… That would mean that Gretel knew Han was in town, and didn't tell me.*

Before Roxy could open her mouth to voice this thought, another two pairs of shoes appeared in the gap. One was the canary-yellow cowboy boots belonging to Solomon Sax. The second was a pair of plain black trainers, loosely laced with a slightly apologetic air.

Roxy might not have seen her brother in person for five years, but she knew – she just *knew* – that these belonged to Han.

"I was actually hoping to speak to my brother in private," came Gretel's voice, sharply. "If that isn't too much to ask."

"Chill out, babe!" came Sax's American twang from somewhere up above the cowboy boots. "It's a party! Turn that frown upside down."

"Oh, I am nobody's *babe*, Sax." Gretel's tone was withering; if Roxy hadn't been so angry with her right now, she'd have been impressed. "And my brother can speak for himself."

"Hey, don't mind me! If Han wants a few minutes to catch up with his big sis—"

"We're *twins*," interrupted Gretel, icily.

"I'm actually older than her," came Han's voice, wryly amused, "by nine and a half minutes."

"Don't let me interrupt a cosy family reunion!" chuckled Sax. "And *all* the Humperdincks are here tonight, it seems!"

Roxy froze. This was it. He was going to tell them he'd seen their little sister being let into the party only five minutes ago. And Gretel was going to find out that Roxy's story about "going to a friend's place to do homework" was nothing but a lie, and she was going to discover that Roxy was on another forbidden adventure, and she was going to be *furious*…

"You're not going to throw up, are you?" Jones hissed, staring across the crawl space directly into Roxy's face. "Because you look like you're going to throw up…"

"Look, Sol," came Han's voice, "give us some time alone, yeah? I'm sure there must be at least *one* girl at this party you haven't tried to chat up yet." His tone was affectionate. "So go and find her, and leave Gretel and me in peace for a bit."

Roxy felt the sick feeling being washed away by a tide of relief. Such relief, in fact, that she didn't even pay attention to the niggling thought that had just crept in at the corner of her mind: *Han and Gretel probably didn't notice what Sax just said because they don't think of anyone else being part of the Humperdinck family…*

"Sure," Sax was saying. "But I'll be right over there, buddy, on the dance floor. If you need me."

Roxy could practically feel Gretel's fury through the mattress above their heads as she watched the canary-yellow cowboy boots swivel and strut away.

"Right," came Gretel's voice, no longer icy but low and tense. "I came as soon as I got your text. What the *flipping* heck are you doing here, Han?"

"It's good to see you, too, G," said Han, mildly, in the tone of someone who was well used to Gretel's intensity. "But I thought I told you to meet me *tomorrow*, and at the hotel, not here…"

"Are you *kidding me*?" Gretel practically screeched, then lowered her voice again, so low this time that

Roxy and Jones had to crane their necks and strain their ears to hear. "You can't still be in Illustria tomorrow, Han! You have to get the first flight out of here *tonight*! Take a private plane, a helicopter if you need to. Don't rock stars do that sort of thing all the time?"

"Sis, come on, I have an album to launch…"

Gretel blew a loud raspberry (which Jones seemed to enjoy). "You've launched a dozen albums before, and you've never felt the need to come back to Illustria to do so!"

"Yeah, but this time, Sol thought it would be nice to—"

"Oh, I might have *known* something as witless as this would be *his* idea!" Gretel's eye-roll was practically audible.

"Don't blame Sol," said Han. "He just thought it would be good for us all to be home here in Illustria for this launch. I mean, it's not like *he* knows we have to be extra careful because of the Law of Sev—" He stopped, abruptly.

"Ha!" Gretel sounded triumphant. "So you *do* remember what I've tried to drum into you about the Law of Sevens!"

Under the Bali water bed, Roxy stared at Jones. Jones stared at Roxy.

"*What's the Law of Sevens?*" Roxy mouthed.

Before Jones could reply, there came a gruesome squelching sound from right above their heads, and – without any warning – two huge bulges appeared in the mattress.

"They've sat down!" hissed Jones, who had the misfortune of being at the southern end of the larger of the two bulges and was now pressed so flat against the floor that she was having to talk out of one corner of her mouth. "And it's a blooming water mattress!"

Roxy, pretty squashed herself, could not actually find the breath to reply.

"You know I can look after myself," came Han's voice from directly above her head. "Anyway, I'm so glad you came tonight. It's really good to see you, G."

"Don't change the subject!" snapped Gretel.

"How's Roxy?" Han went on, blithely ignoring her. "All good?"

"*Roxy?*" Gretel sounded momentarily baffled. "Oh, she's fine, I guess. She seems to have settled into life in Rexopolis. And she's safely back under her False Memory Enchantment, at least, after that ridiculous stunt she pulled with Queen Bellissima."

"Be fair, G." There was a grin in Han's voice. "Turning the evil Queen into a giant vegan muffin was kind of an awesome move."

"It was silly and childish, and she had absolutely no idea what she was messing with," Gretel retorted.

"Come on. She's just a kid," said Han.

"Will you stop changing the subject? There are more important things to discuss right now than our little sister!"

"*Ouch*," mouthed Jones at Roxy, who was starting to wish that the squelchy bulge above would just flatten her entirely. It was bad enough that her brother and sister had arranged to meet and kept her well out of the way, but hearing them describe her as *just a kid*, and not important enough to discuss … it was mortifying.

"And what's important –" Gretel had never cared for chit-chat – "is you and me. And the Law of Sevens. And that's why you have to leave Illustria, Han. You have to leave tonight."

There it was again – this *Law of Sevens*. Whatever it was, merely talking about it was clearly agitating Gretel so much that the bulge above Jones's head – presumably a bulge created by Gretel's bottom – was wobbling and wibbling. This was very bad news for Jones, who was now rather desperately trying to commando-crawl backwards towards the plant stalk, to avoid having her entire face flattened like a pancake.

"You know the witch is still out there," Gretel was going on, her voice cracking. "We might not know where she is or what she's planning, but we know that whatever it is, she'll want to get her hands on both of us…"

*The witch*, Roxy knew all too well, was the Gingerbread Witch, who had lured Han and Gretel into her cottage in the woods when they were just children. This had all been spun into a fairytale by the Story-Weavers – the people employed by the Soup Ministry to cover up any trace of Illustria's murky magical past – but the fact was that it had all really happened. This was one of the many brand-new pieces of knowledge that Roxy had been determined Mrs Smith's False Memory Enchantment would not take away. Unpleasant though it was to know about this terrible part of her brother and sister's past, she would still rather know than not. It helped her to understand that feeling she had always had, of being on the outside of her half-siblings' intensely private relationship.

It was a feeling that, right now, was burning so fiercely inside her that she thought it might be about to devour her, just like the Gingerbread Witch could have eaten up Hansel and Gretel. *There are important things to discuss*, Gretel had said, *and what's important is you and me…* Even if Roxy could understand it better these days, it didn't make it any easier to accept.

Jones, by now, had managed to squirm all the way to the end of the bed to the very back of the crawl space, up to the plant stalk. In fact, Roxy suddenly noticed, it looked almost as if she had managed to squirm somewhat *into* the plant stalk, but that couldn't be right … could it?

"Jeez, Louise!" Jones hissed, her startled eyes latching on to Roxy's as the two of them realized the same thing at once. "There's a gap down here… Oh my stars!" she suddenly yelped, catching sight of something.

The voices above them stopped.

"Did you just hear that?" Roxy heard Gretel say.

"Hear what?" asked Han.

"It sounded like someone talking," Gretel replied.

"Um, you do know this is a party, G?" Han's voice sounded amused. "Talking is kind of what happens."

"Oh, for heaven's sake! I meant it sounded like someone talking *under the bed*," said Gretel, irritably. "Let me just check this out."

The mattress was moving. Gretel was standing up. There wasn't time for Roxy to follow Jones before Gretel peered down and saw her.

Instinctively, Roxy fumbled in the shoulder bag to

find the tiny pocket where the Witching Stone grit was nestled. Pulling the fragment out, she pointed it at the mattress.

"*Aperstatus Hexaflor*," she hissed, which – in her panic – were the only magic words she could actually remember, and which – she realized as soon as she had spoken them – were from the ridiculous online spell provider Jones had subscribed her to, and were intended for the opening-up of tricky jam jars or stuck windows. They would obviously do no good whatsoever in this entirely jamless and windowless crisis…

But two things happened, a split second apart. First, the fragment suddenly became so searingly hot that Roxy nearly dropped it. Second, a cascade of water came down on top of her head.

"The mattress!" shrieked Gretel, as both bulges above scrabbled off the collapsing mattress. "*Stupid* water beds…"

Roxy managed to scramble backwards through the gap in the stalk before Gretel remembered that she'd been about to investigate.

"Check this out," Jones said, in awed tones, as a gasping, soaked Roxy joined her on the inside. "It's only a blooming *lift*."

**5**

The inside of the giant plant stalk looked, astonishingly, like the kind of large, circular lobby you might find in a smart hotel. It was quiet in here – muffled, almost; the hubbub of the party, just on the other side of the stalk, sounded miles away rather than mere metres. The smooth curved walls were a glossy dark green, and the floor was thickly carpeted to match.

And there really was a lift, right there in the centre of the lobby – burnished metallic green, with ornate green-and-gold filigreed doors.

"Oh, we are *so* getting in this. Awesome magic, by the way!" Jones gave Roxy a double thumbs up as she stepped towards the lift. "Didn't I tell you *Basic Incantations at Thy Fingertips* would come in handy? You're totally soaked, by the way, did you know?"

"I'd noticed, thanks." Roxy's scratchy blue lace was

even scratchier now that it was also sopping wet and rather cold. "I ... I still can't believe that spell worked!"

"And didn't I tell you there was a secret entrance to SkyZone in the nightclub, Roxy? *Didn't I?* This has to be it!" Jones pressed a green button beside the lift doors and waited, impatiently hopping from foot to foot. "Why won't it open?"

"SkyZone pass required," came a smooth computerized female voice from the lift. "Please show SkyZone pass for entry to Lift B."

"I haven't got a SkyZone pass!" Jones howled. "You don't have one, do you?"

"Why on earth would I have a *SkyZone pass*?" Roxy glanced, anxiously, over her soggy shoulder. "Jones, my sister might find her way in here at any moment..."

"All the more reason to get these lift doors open! Oh, wait." Jones suddenly whirled round, pointing a finger at Roxy. "*You* can get these doors open!"

"But I said already, I don't have a pass!"

"Not with a *pass*! With a *spell*." Jones grabbed the fragment of Stone that Roxy was still clutching in her damp hands. "Use this again! It worked on that water mattress, didn't it?"

"Jones, I don't think..."

"We don't need you to *think*." Jones pressed the grit firmly back into Roxy's hand. "We need you to *do*."

Roxy's fingers automatically curled around the grit – or, as she was now thinking of it, with an important capital: the Grit. It was cool again, and perfectly smooth to the touch, and it felt like something her hand had been missing.

"All right." She cleared her throat. "I'll try. But you'd better stand back, Jones."

"Ooooh, d'you really think it will be that powerful?" Jones's eyes gleamed. She took a small step backwards, poised to leap through the lift doors when – *if* – they slid open. "Go on, then, kiddo. Do your stuff!"

Roxy took a deep breath, closed her eyes and cast her mind back to the spell she'd read on her phone just the other day. There had been some kind of preamble; maybe saying this out loud would help.

"*Need a stubborn window opened? Or a cupboard, or a door? This will break the blockage:* **Aperstatus Hexaflor!**" Roxy lifted the Grit as she spoke, and wafted it vaguely, almost apologetically, in the direction of the lift.

Suddenly, the Grit was hot again. So burning hot that she almost dropped it. But, to her amazement, it had worked. The lift doors were opening.

"Welcome to Lift B," came the smooth computerized voice again. "Please embark and prepare for immediate departure."

"Go!" gasped Jones, pulling Roxy through the doors

with her only a moment before they slid smoothly shut again. "Whoo-hoo!" she added, punching the air with excitement as the lift began to rise. "You did it, kiddo!"

"I did it," murmured Roxy, gazing around them. The fact she'd just successfully performed a magic spell – for the second time in as many minutes – was less astounding to her than the fact they were travelling up in a lift *on the inside of a plant stalk*. "Jones, I don't get it," she said. "The nightclub was on the very top of Snelling's, right?"

"Yeah. I mean, the clue's in the name, Rox: *Roof* Garden. Why?"

"Well, if we were just on a rooftop, how can we be going up … and up … and up?" In fact, Roxy was starting to feel rather queasy: the lift was not only continuing to rise, but was gathering speed. She gripped on to the rail that ran around the inside – like everything else inside the lift, it was green and highly polished. "If there's a massive stalk this tall coming out of the top of Snelling's, don't you think people would notice?"

"It's probably concealed with magic," said Jones. "A powerful Invisibility Charm, I'll bet! If they want to keep this SkyZone place hidden, a magical lift up to it is a pretty smart solution."

"So you think it's a *magical* lift, then?" Roxy asked,

nervously. "You don't think there are safer things involved, like – you know – actual engineering?"

"You know, this is all part of your problem." Jones sat down, cross-legged, on the lift floor, and opened up the front pocket of her kitbag. She took out a handful of mini hot-dog canapés – when had she managed to swipe *these* from the party? – and began to munch, contentedly. "You never just relax and go with the flow. You're still asking too many questions. But when you stop doing that, and trust your instincts instead – well, that spell with the water mattress back there was *inspired*! Talk about getting one over on your sister!"

"I don't want to talk about my sister, thanks," said Roxy, busying herself by carefully replacing the Grit in the inner pocket of the (slightly soggy) satin bag.

"Oh. Right. No. Of course."

"I mean, she obviously knew Han was coming home for the first time in years, but clearly neither of them wanted me to see him."

"Well, that's got to hurt."

"Mind you, seeing as they obviously think I'm nothing but some silly, embarrassing, completely unimportant kid, why *would* they want me to see him?"

"Uh-huh."

70

"And as we both clearly heard, they only care about each other, so—"

"Look, do you actually want to talk about this after all?" Jones said, through a mouthful of hot dog. "Because I thought you just said you didn't, but now here you are going on and on and on about it…"

"I don't want to talk about it," Roxy muttered. "You're right. Let's just forget it."

"I mean," Jones went on, blithely, "I don't think there's anything *personal* about your brother and sister taking absolutely zero interest in you."

"Thanks for that."

"It's obvious that they've got some info about that horrible witch. And you can hardly blame them for getting all super-paranoid about *that*." Jones kindly held out a mini hot-dog, but Roxy waved it away. The mere thought of food made her feel sicker than ever.

"So what was she even talking about back there?" she asked, shortly, not wanting to mention Gretel's name. "All that *Law of Sevens* stuff. Do you know anything about that?"

"Not much." Jones swallowed her hot dog and reached back into her kitbag to pull out her leather notebook (and another hot dog). There was a loud snore from Mirror inside: it sounded as if it was out for the count. "The phrase rings a bell, though. Let me see…" She flipped through several pages, frowning as she read aloud. *"Three Little Pigs Conspiracy… Golden Goose: might it actually have laid edible golden eggs…? Who were those bizarre elves who kept popping up at night and making shoes for some old shoemaker. I mean, that's just weird, right…?* Oh, here we are! *The Law of Sevens.* Yeah, I remember now, I read about it somewhere in Dad's notes… *Sounds like a bad thing,"* she read from her own scribbles, her tangerine hair flopping over her face. *"Something to do with a Diabolical power upsurge. Find out more about it when you have time and when your stupid stepsisters stop asking you to do stupid things like handwash their stupid silk sleep-masks or arrange their stupid nail polishes in ascending order of pinkness—"*

"Please be advised," interrupted the lift, in its sultry voice, "we will shortly reach altitude of one thousand five hundred metres. Expect sensations of ear-popping and mild light-headedness."

"We're *one and a half kilometres* up?" croaked Roxy, gripping the rail tighter than ever. "How is this possible, Jones? What kind of a plant stalk even *grows* this tall?"

"Oh my stars!" Jones whacked the floor so hard that the sausage flew out of her hot dog and bounced off the lift doors. *"I* know what plant stalk grows this tall! *Jack's."*

"As in … *and the Beanstalk*?" Roxy asked. "That Jack?"

"That exact Jack! I should have worked it out before! *Obviously* the giant beanstalk still exists! It's not the kind of thing you can get rid of easily. Especially not if there's a secret government lab you quite fancy housing somewhere super-inaccessible!"

"So you think this SkyZone place is a secret lab?"

"It's precisely what I think it is! Dad had a few random scribbles in his notes, but I never thought much about it until I found those papers in the attic. He was sure there had to be a place where MOOOOOH could try out whatever Magiscience they wanted, well away from prying eyes."

"Magiscience?" echoed Roxy. "What on earth is Magiscience?"

"Kind of a hybrid of magic and science." Jones was tucking into her third mini hot dog. "Frankie mentioned it once, when he – actually, *she*, back then – was wondering how to make alterations to a spell that didn't seem to be working. It's called *exspellimentation*, Frankie told me. Come to think of it, he could probably do with a good old exspelliment right now, if he's still stuck looking like a ten-year-old boy rather than a three-hundred-and-sixty-four-year-old fairy!"

"But what has SkyZone, or these … *exspelliments*,

or whatever they're called…" Roxy pinched her nose for a second, and blew hard to try to counteract the growing pressure in her ears, "got to do with this missing thing you *still* haven't explained?"

"Ooooh, yes, I forgot I need to tell you about that!" Jones uncrossed her legs and lolled, with great satisfaction, on the green glass floor. "Think about it, Roxy. What went missing, in the bad old days of the Cursed Kingdom, and *never, ever, ever* came back?"

Roxy blinked at her.

"Or let me rephrase that!" Jones lifted both hands and mimed something, inexpertly. It might have been *tickling a drainpipe* or *scratching a banana*. "*Who* went missing, and never, ever, ever came back?"

Which – no thanks at all to Jones's rubbish mime – was when Roxy got it. A tingle of something – nerves, excitement – went up her spine. "You were miming playing a pipe! Are you talking about the children that danced away to the tune of the Pied Piper? *That's* who we're looking for?"

Jones grinned. "Yep. They danced away and never returned, pretty much exactly the same way it happens in the so-called fairytale. You remember the Story-Weavers, right?"

"Yeah," said Roxy. "I remember them. They were the specialist department within MOOOOOH who

74

rewrote the Cursed Kingdom's history during the Great Clean-Up."

"Exactly!" said Jones. "With the help of the False Memory Enchantment, they made it sound as though all the bad things that had happened in the kingdom were just made up fairytales, to tell to children at bedtime. Well, obviously they got stuck into the whole Pied Piper thing straight after the Great Clean-Up – in fact, the whole Pied Piper thing was the main reason for the Great Clean-Up. Three hundred kids going missing all at once was the moment people in Illustria decided enough was enough with the Dark Magic."

"So all those children really did just follow some piper all the way to a mountain that sealed up behind them?"

"Exactly." Jones stuck up a thumb. "The Weavers might have changed a few details here and there, but they usually stick as close to the truth as they possibly can. Lies are more convincing that way. Anyway, that's what I reckon Susan Little was trying to tell people about, that night she appeared at the Roof Garden. I think she worked at SkyZone, which must be how she knew about the Missing. And I think that she must have become angry, over time, that they were being kept hidden away from their families just so that nobody would accidentally remember anything about the kingdom's dark past. I mean, False Memory Enchantments aren't perfect, you know. Sometimes old memories slip through the cracks – especially if a painful enough reminder is given."

Roxy could feel a growing horror spreading all the way through her body. "What on earth do their *families* think happened to them?"

Jones thought about this for a moment. "I'll bet, as well as the plain old False Memory Enchantment, they'll have had another strong enchantment put on them so they never even remember they had kids at all. Let's face it, any time there's a danger of people finding out the truth, that's what the Ministry do – bung a massive enchantment on them."

"That's so sad." Roxy swallowed, hard. "That would mean those children have been … completely forgotten."

"But that's where we come in! Imagine it, Roxy – for over two decades, those kids have been trapped deep in some hidden mountain, never knowing if they'll see the light of day again … and then, like a knight in shining armour, enter Jones –" Jones thrust a triumphant fist into the air, eyes gleaming – "and Roxy, obviously," she added. "But my point is, we're going to *do something about it*."

Roxy could not have said why, but these words had made her shiver.

"You've gone all bug-eyed and weird," Jones pointed out, getting to her feet and hoiking her kitbag onto her shoulders. The lift was slowing down. "You're not worrying about giants, are you?"

"Why would I be worrying about giants?"

"Oh, you know –" Jones waved a hand – "because of the whole giant-at-the-top-of-the-beanstalk thing."

"Wait. You don't think …"

"Lift is slowing down," announced the voice, pleasantly. "Please prepare for imminent arrival at SkyZone."

"… that we're going to be met by some kind of giant…?" Roxy continued.

"We thank you for choosing Lift B for your journey today," the lift voice went on. "It is unlikely that you will find yourself suffering from the symptoms of altitude sickness whilst at SkyZone, but if you begin to suffer from a headache or find yourself with a nasty nosebleed, please make your way immediately to the Hospital Wing on level six. Maps are available in the main foyer. And, for your comfort and relaxation, please remember that SkyZone has been one hundred per cent man-eating-giant-free since the eleventh of March 1822. Have a pleasant day!"

"Hear that? Man-eating-giant-*free*! *And* it's highly unlikely that we'll get altitude sickness! So really, there's absolutely nothing to worry about."

"Oh, there's *always* something to worry about," muttered Roxy, as the lift drew to a halt, and the doors slid smoothly open.

**6**

Roxy and Jones stepped into what looked like the Great Hall of a vast stone castle.

A vaulted ceiling stretched hundreds of metres above their heads. The dark grey flagstone floor stretched so far in every direction that you couldn't see where it ended; indeed, the giant single flagstone the pair were standing on was itself the length and width of a tennis court. There were narrow slits for windows, high above their heads, that looked exactly the sort of thing an angry giant might have leaned out of to pour massive vats of boiling oil over unwanted visitors. The walls were covered in richly woven but faded tapestries featuring woodland scenes: stags the size of double-deckers and trees as big as houses. There were massive stone pillars, too, reaching neck-craning distances up to touch the ceiling, and Jones pulled Roxy behind one of these only a moment after the doors of Lift B closed smoothly shut behind them.

"Hide!" Jones hissed. "Magiscientists!"

Roxy was just about to ask Jones how she knew what a Magiscientist even looked like when she saw what Jones was jabbing her finger at. A couple of flagstones away – which was so far that Roxy had to strain her eyes to get a proper view through the growing dusk – a little huddle of mercifully non-gigantic people were swiftly and silently crossing the Great Hall. They were all wearing silver-white robes – like the lab coats that ordinary scientists might wear, but longer and more flowing, and with wide sticking-up collars that obscured their faces – and they were almost all carrying heavy books and overflowing piles of paper. Some of them were extremely short and squat, looking even at this distance quite like Skinny, the angry gnome the girls had befriended on their last mission; others looked precisely as willowy and elegant as Mortadella, the reformed evil fairy who now ran a wellness retreat in Sleeping Beauty's old castle. But even if these similarities didn't convince Roxy that the group were all BOBIs, there was another clue: they weren't only carrying books and papers.

"Are those *wands*?" she hissed.

"Of course they're wands! What else do you

expect them to do exspelliments with? The more important question," Jones murmured, "is where are they all heading? I mean, they look like they're going *somewhere*, right?"

Jones had a point; the Magiscientists looked purposeful. Then Roxy saw something extraordinary. The Magiscientists had reached the centre of the Great Hall, from where, quite suddenly and without any warning, they began to *rise*.

"They're flying!" she gasped.

"Don't be ridiculous," Jones snorted. "They're not flying. They're levitating."

"Because that's *totally* different!" Roxy said, in exasperation, but Jones was ignoring her, intently watching the Magiscientists.

They were flying – all right, *levitating* – higher and higher above the middle of the Hall. And as they ascended, they began to peel off, two or three at a time. They appeared to float to the walls and then hover outside non-giant-sized doorways, each painted plain black and with absolutely no distinguishing features. A moment later, these doors would open up, and the Magiscientists would float through as they closed smoothly behind them.

"Those'll be their labs," Jones whispered, although as far as Roxy could tell, there was absolutely no hard evidence that labs were behind the doors. "We absolutely have to get into one of those, Roxy! That's where we'll find out exactly what happens here!"

Roxy pulled Jones further back behind their pillar, worried that they could be seen from this angle by some of the straggling BOBIs. "And how exactly do you suggest we get *into* any of the labs, rooms, whatever, up there, Jones? Last time I checked, neither of us had the ability to levitate."

Jones frowned, thinking for a moment. Then her face cleared. "You can do a spell with the Grit!"

"Jones, the only two spells I have even the faintest clue how to work are one that opens jam jars – well, OK, apparently lift doors, too, oh, and water mattresses – and one that… Oh." Roxy stared back at Jones. "One that can *fly your shopping bags home from the supermarket*."

"Exacta-rama!" Jones beamed the kind of beam she only beamed when they were about to try something ridiculously reckless. "If you can make shopping bags fly, you can make us fly!"

"Levitate."

"Don't split hairs." Seeing that the last of the Magiscientists had now disappeared behind their doors, Jones hauled Roxy out from behind the pillar and led the way to the centre of the now-deserted

Hall. It took two or three minutes of speed-walking to get there, their footsteps echoing eerily on the flagstones as they went. "Right," Jones said, tilting her head back at a sharp angle and peering up at the walls high above. "Now, let's not get cocky. First time with this spell, you'll probably only be able to take us up – what? Thirty metres? Forty?"

"I don't even know if I'll be able to get us *one* metre in the air!" Roxy sighed at Jones, already reaching for the Grit in her pocket. "Can we just be realistic?"

Jones blew a loud raspberry. "You can do anything you set your mind to, Roxy Humperdinck. I'd give it a shot myself, but for some unfathomable reason the Grit seems to like you more than me. So you need to tell yourself you can magic us *three hundred* metres into the air. Shoot for the stars. Aim high. Stop being such a whingy-whiny-mingy-moany Negative Nelly, for once, and…"

Roxy had just opened her mouth to thank Jones for the inspiring pep talk when something sharp hit her – *thwack!* – right between the eyebrows.

"Ouch! What was that?" she gasped, just as Jones yelped and put a hand to the back of her head.

"Someone's firing at us!" Jones spun round.

Someone was gesturing at them from behind one of the pillars, halfway across the Hall.

It was a boy.

Even at this distance, it was clear that he was just a plain old ordinary boy, and not a Magiscientist or any other kind of BOBI. He was tall, and wearing jeans and a burgundy hoodie, and by the increasingly frantic sweeps of his arms it looked like he was trying to warn them about something. Then he finally cupped his hands around his mouth and called, "You can't do magic here!"

Roxy and Jones blinked back at him, too surprised to reply.

"Not unless you want every single Magiscientist in this place to come running!" he added, at a yell. "Or one of the... Oh, this is ridiculous. I'm coming over." The boy dropped his hands and began to jog, at speed, towards them.

"Should we run?" Jones hissed at Roxy, uncertain for once.

"No ... yes ... I don't know... He doesn't look dangerous... He looks..."

Roxy stopped, now that the boy had almost reached them.

He was about twelve or thirteen, with ink-black hair that swept right down into eyes of melted chocolate. He had a chiselled jaw and a nose that could have been sculpted by Michelangelo.

Up until now, Jones had probably been the best-looking person Roxy had ever seen, but this boy made even Jones look a bit average.

"... or one of the security patrols," he finished. "They know when unauthorized spells are being performed." He grabbed Jones by the elbow. "You both need to come with me. They might show up at any moment."

"Oi! Let go of me!" Jones wrestled her arm free. "We're not coming with you! We don't even know who you are."

"I'm Charley," said the boy. "*Now* will you come with me?"

"Don't be ridic—" Jones began.

"Look, we don't mean to be impolite or anything," Roxy said, interrupting her, "but where exactly do you want to take us?"

"Well, we could stand around debating whether you fancy a tour of the library or a freezing dip in the lake," Charley said, pushing a handful of hair out of exasperated eyes. "Or you could just trust that I know what I'm talking about and..." He stopped. "Oh, *great*."

It did not sound like a positive *great*.

"OK, there's no time to explain," Charley went on, jerking his head across the Hall.

A group of people were heading in their direction.

"Magiscientists?" Roxy hissed.

"No… Look, just go along with everything I say, all right? And don't talk too much," Charley added, eyeing Jones rather pointedly.

"Hey, I've hardly said a—"

"Ssssh. They're coming." As the group drew closer, Charley altered his posture to appear deliberately casual. "Hey, Brian G," he called out. "What's up?"

Brian G, Roxy decided, must be the harassed-looking man at the front. He was wearing a neon-orange T-shirt and acid-green shorts, and a big, bright badge on his chest declaring that it was **TIME TO HAVE FUN!** Behind him trailed a dozen or so children, who did not look like they agreed with the badge. They ranged in age from about seven to about thirteen: a mixture of boys and girls, all wearing the same hoodie as Charley, just in differing shades – burgundy or navy for the boys, bottle green or grey for the girls. It was hard to work out exactly what they were doing up here. The hoodies didn't look smart enough to be a school uniform – and anyway, what kind of crazy school trip brought you to a giant's castle thousands of metres in the sky? They must be the children of people working here at SkyZone, Roxy thought. Perhaps the hoodies signified some kind of official workplace childcare, the sort of thing Roxy's various uninterested stepmothers had so often tried to persuade her dad to put Roxy in – for as many after-school hours as possible.

"Hey there, Charley," Brian G replied, as the children shuffled their feet behind him. "What are you doing out here in the Hall?" Then, catching sight of Roxy and Jones, "And why aren't you two girls wearing your Fun Activity Time clothes?"

Roxy froze. Jones opened her mouth just as Charley spoke.

"Oh, they got paint on their hoodies in Amazing Art Club," he said, in the same smooth tone that Jones used when she was lying. "They were just on their way to Laundry to get fresh ones."

"I see." Brian G did not seem interested enough in either Jones or Roxy to pursue it. "But, Charley, aren't you meant to be in Maggie G's Film Appreciation Club right now?"

"Not today," Charley replied, glibly. "Maggie gave me permission to skip it. I was just heading to the library to do some extra work on my Enchanted Household Objects project."

"That's good to hear, lad!" Brian G tried to inject some enthusiasm into his voice, and gave Charley a double thumbs up. "Great to see you applying yourself! Especially after your recent behaviour…"

"Hey, I thought nobody was going to mention that,"

said a stocky boy at the front of the group. He was wearing a burgundy hoodie exactly like Charley's, and was cheerfully working his way through a packet of crisps. "Director Humperdinck made it clear she wasn't angry with me or Charley about the whole sneaking-into-her-office incident …"

At the words *Director Humperdinck*, Roxy very nearly let out a squeak, contained only by Jones stamping her foot firmly down on her left toes.

"… especially as we didn't even find anything interesting in there," the boy was going on, through a mouthful of crisps. "Carob-covered macadamia nuts was about as exciting as it got."

If there had been the slightest doubt in Roxy's mind that Director Humperdinck was Gretel, the mention of carob-covered macadamias dispelled it immediately. They were her sugar-phobic sister's favourite "treat", despite – or maybe because of – the fact they looked and tasted like three-day-old rabbit droppings.

"Yeah, anyway," Charley was saying, giving the crisp-eating boy exactly the kind of *stop-talking* look he'd recently given Jones. "Don't let me keep you guys. You're on your way to the kitchens for Cool Cookery Club, right?"

"We sure are!" said Brian G, before adding, with more than a hint of desperation in his voice, "Today we're all going to learn how to make our own delicious but healthy pizzas! Won't that be fun, gang?"

Several yawns were stifled; multiple pairs of eyes were rolled.

"Then let's go, team! That means you, too, Sam," Brian G added over his shoulder to the crisp-eating boy, who was dragging his heels as the rest of the group began to troop away across the Great Hall.

"Um, actually, Brian G, now I think about it I might need to go to the library too." Sam was perspiring slightly and shifting from foot to foot; he was clearly about as talented a liar as Roxy. "For, y'know, project work and stuff… Maybe I'll go with Charley and … um … meet you in the kitchens a bit later?"

Brian G was being distracted by a noisy squabble that had broken out among three of his group. He merely waved a hand in Sam's direction, which Sam obviously decided to take as permission.

"So, what's going on?" Sam asked, eagerly, as soon as the group was safely out of earshot. He stared at Roxy and Jones with wide eyes before turning to Charley. "Who are these two?"

"I don't actually know their names," began Charley. "But it looks like they're a couple of princesses or someth—"

"Hey! We're not *princesses*!" Jones practically spat

the word. "I'm Trudie Splashback and this is Araminta Ponsonby-Pikelet, and we happen to be *adventurers*. In disguise."

"Yeah?" Charley raised an unconvinced eyebrow, then stared down at Jones. "You're kind of short to be an *adventurer*, aren't you?"

"Hey, listen, buddy…"

"Anyway, the fancy frocks are handy if we bump into anyone else on our way up to the dorms," Charley went on, taking Jones by the elbow and beckoning Sam and Roxy to follow. "You can just pretend you're on your way to Stella G's Ballroom Dancing Club."

"What *are* all these clubs?" Jones demanded, shaking off Charley's hand. They had reached a narrow stone doorway at the far end of the Great Hall, which led to a flight of spiralling stone steps. They were clearly designed for giants, but were now filled in with three or four smaller ledges to every step. "And who are all these people with the surname G?"

"Oh, they're the giants," said Sam over his shoulder, starting to climb the stairs. "They look after us up here."

"Giants?" Roxy stared up at his round, friendly face (which reminded her, oddly enough, of one of Jones's beloved Custarde Doughnuts). "That guy Brian wasn't a *giant*."

"A *shrunken* giant," Sam went on. "Surely you guys have come across shrunken giants down on the ground?"

"Sam!" Charley exclaimed. "Will you shut up? We don't even know they're *from* down on the ground!"

"Well, where else could they be from?" Sam sounded indignant. "They're not from *up here*! I've never seen either of them before. And I can *definitely* remember as far back as three years ago now, because—"

"I said shut UP!" Charley's cheeks were flushed, though it was possible that this was simply from the exertion of climbing the seemingly never-ending staircase. "They could be anyone! They could be ..."

"... spies?" Jones filled in the word. "We're not. But what was that about a dorm? You don't *live* up here, do you?"

"Course we live up here," Sam puffed. "Where else would we live? This is—"

"Sam, I swear on Rexopolis United, if you don't stop talking RIGHT NOW..." Charley broke off, mid-threat, as they finally reached the top of the staircase.

They were in a flagstone corridor now, so dimly lit that Roxy could not even see Jones's expression as the pair of them followed the two boys. Several doors led off the corridor, but Charley kept going all the way to the end to an arched wooden door marked with the word **CLOUDBURST**.

"OK, we don't really allow girls to visit," he said. "But that's girls from Sunshine, Rainbow and Snowfall dorms. I think we can make an exception as you're not from *any* dorm."

The huge, high-ceilinged room Roxy and Jones were ushered into was quite evidently a dormitory itself. Even more evidently, it was a dormitory belonging to a bunch of *boys*. Dozens of boys, Roxy worked out, going by the number of unmade beds and wardrobes with football posters on them. Someone had (probably) been using a couple of these as goalposts, because they were pretty battered and covered in ball-shaped dents. Along the walls were a few faintly unsanitary washbasins, crowded with toothbrushes and murky-looking flannels, and in a mirror above one basin a ridiculous moustachioed face had been drawn in soap.

"Shouldn't we still get them to swear an oath, Charley?" Sam was already scurrying to one of the beds, right by a tall, latticed window that only looked narrow because it was three times as high as it was wide (in fact, it was as wide as Jones and Roxy lying down end to end). He reached under the pillow and produced an extremely dog-eared Rexopolis

United football annual. It was actually curling up at the corners, which Roxy had never seen a hardback book do before, and from the date – twenty-two years previously – it was clearly an actual antique, in football annual terms, at least. "They could swear on this to prove that they're not spies, and that they won't go straight to Director Humperdinck and tell her everything we know. Not that I'm saying you're lying," Sam added, apologetically, to Roxy and Jones. "But we can't be too careful, especially now we know they've actually *imprisoned* somebody in the room next door."

"Imprisoned?" croaked Roxy.

"Yeah, and we've been communicating with the prisoner by tapping on the wall, like people do in books and stuff! It's difficult to understand much, because they seem a bit confused by our code—"

Sam stopped, very suddenly, because Charley had just picked up a pillow and thrown it very hard at his head.

"What's wrong with you?" Charley yelled. "Fifteen seconds ago you were worrying about them being spies, and now you're blabbing *everything we know*!"

"Oh." Sam looked crestfallen. He reached underneath his bed and pulled out a large handful of crisp bags, one of which he pulled open. "That's a good point," he said, through a mournful mouthful. "Sorry."

"But we're *not* spies," Roxy said, wanting to make Sam feel better.

"Yeah, yeah, you're *adventurers*." Charley rolled his eyes. "Adventurers with suspiciously fake-sounding names."

"Hey, they're not fake!" said Jones, sitting down cross-legged on Sam's bed and helping herself to a packet of crisps. "Anyway, who says *you're* not going by a fake name?" she went on, glaring up at Charley. "How are we supposed to trust you? You've just dragged us up here without telling us anything at all! You haven't told us what a whole bunch of kids are doing, living up here at SkyZone. You haven't explained about any of those awful Fun Activity clubs, or why you're all wearing these creepy hoodies … and now we learn there's an actual *prisoner* in the room next door! I mean, what the blooming heck is going on around here?"

"And who's this *Director* you mentioned?" Roxy couldn't help asking, despite the glare it earned her from Jones. "Director of what? We thought this was a laboratory, but now it seems like maybe it's some kind of … boarding school, or something?"

"Well, we do lessons and stuff," Sam replied, cheerfully. "But I don't know if it counts as an actual boarding school. I mean, when you're at a boarding school, you go home for holidays and stuff, right? Whereas none of us has been home for the last twenty years…"

This time he stopped himself before a pillow-missile could even reach him.

"Sorry, Charley. My bad."

"OK, OK." Charley raked a hand through his hair. He looked like he was fighting to stay calm. "Maybe you could just … forget he said that?" he asked Roxy and Jones, desperately. "Or at least you could look a *bit* less freaked out?"

"But that didn't even make any sense," Jones began. "How can you possibly have lived here for the last *twenty years*? You're no older than I am!"

"And you're – what?" A hint of a cheeky smile was creeping back into Charley's dark eyes. "Eight? Nine?"

"She's thirteen!" Roxy said, hastily, before Jones could erupt. "But, Charley, you can't expect us to believe you're both *twenty*."

"Sam never said we were twenty." Charley sat down on another of the unmade beds for a moment. He looked tired, suddenly. "Actually, I'm almost thirty-three. And Sam is…"

"Thirty-one last month," Sam announced.

"OK, very funny." Jones narrowed her eyes at them both. "Remind me again who was the one accusing us of having fake-sounding *names*? Well, at least we haven't got fake ages. Unless maybe we should join in the fun too – I reckon I could easily pass for forty-six, and my friend Araminta here is so tall I think we could just claim she's fifty-nine…"

Which was when Roxy gave a squeak.

Because she knew *exactly* how Charley could actually be almost thirty-three, and Sam could have been thirty-one last month.

"Don't you get it, Jones? We've found them. Well, two of them, anyway. Charley and Sam – they're the Missing!"

## 7

If Roxy hadn't been struggling with the enormity of this discovery herself, she would have really enjoyed the expression on Jones's face right now. It was an extraordinary mixture of delight (that they had found at least two of the Missing, the whole point of their mission), irritation (that Roxy had been the first one to work it out) and fury (that Charley was one of them).

"Yeah." Charley looked from one to the other of them, warily. "We're the Missing. How do *you* know that?"

"Because you're our mission! You're the reason why we're exploring! Oh, Jones!" Roxy turned to her friend. "Isn't this amazing?"

"Not exactly *amazing*." Jones shrugged. Now that she had mastered her mingled delight and outrage, she

97

was deliberately casual. "We're top adventurers. We *always* find what we're looking for."

"Wait a minute," Sam said, staring at Roxy. "Did you just call her *Jones*?"

"Yeah, big surprise, our names aren't really Trudie Splashback and … well, whatever else I said." Jones waved a hand, unconcerned by being caught out. "I *told* you, Roxy," she went on, triumphantly, "that if we followed Susan Little's trail, we'd find what we were looking for."

"*Susan Little*? How do you know her?" Charley asked, sharply.

"We don't." Jones stared at him. "Do you?"

"It was her name on the message that came on the tiny aeroplane!" Sam was practically hopping with excitement. "We found it on the roof just outside the dorm –" he gestured towards the window – "a few weeks ago."

Roxy was struggling to think what a *tiny aeroplane* could be. "Do you mean … maybe … some kind of drone?"

"Yeah, a drone." Charley's face cleared, as if he'd suddenly remembered a word that had been evading him for ages. "That's what it was."

"Can I show them the message?" Sam asked him, breathlessly. "We can trust them, I reckon. Don't you?"

"I reckon we can trust *her*." Charley nodded in Roxy's direction. "The short one, on the other hand..."

"Hey, I'd rather be short than old," Jones shot back.

"I'd rather be old," Charley retorted, "than—"

"Take a look at this!" Sam interrupted, heading over towards Roxy with a scrap of paper he'd just pulled out from under his pillow. "Charley and I were lying awake one night – he'd started having these nightmares, you see, shouting out names in his sleep and stuff – well, one name again and again, to be more accurate, *Charmian*—"

"Girlfriend?" Jones broke in.

"I don't have a girlfriend." Charley glared at her. "Certainly not one called Charmian."

"Someone you've got a massive crush on, then?" Jones nodded, maddeningly certain. "One of the girls you've been with here at SkyZone for twenty years."

"No! Look, I don't even know anyone called Charmian! And Sam, *please* –" Charley turned his irritation to his roommate – "I'd prefer it if you didn't go around spilling *all* my personal information to people we've only just met?"

"Right. Course. Anyway –" Sam seemed eager to carry on with his story – "we were trying to stay awake so Charley wouldn't yell in his sleep and wake up the other guys in the dorm... And then we heard this noise from outside, so we opened the window and saw this little, what did you call it, *drone* thing. We hauled it in and found this attached."

Roxy looked down at the crumpled-up piece of paper he'd handed her and read aloud the scribbled message.

"*To anyone who finds this near the SkyZone dormitories: please do not be alarmed. This is from a friend. You are being kept at SkyZone because they do not want to tell you THE TRUTH: that you followed the evil Pied Piper many years ago and were led all the way to a hidden cave deep within the Deadwoods...*"

"Let me see that!" Jones peered over Roxy's lacy shoulder. "*After several months,*" she continued to read, "*you escaped and were eventually found by official scouts, wandering the Woods. When it was discovered that the Piper had put you under a powerful Ever-Youth Charm that COULD NOT BE BROKEN, you were brought to SkyZone so that experts could work on a cure. You have been ENCHANTED to forget all of this, and your families have been ENCHANTED to forget you, to conceal our country's magical past! But you deserve BETTER. You must DEMAND to be told the whole truth. Really hope they're getting closer to finding a cure, by the way. Also, hope the food's improved. There were lots of awful biscuits when I was there. Giants are rubbish at biscuits. I'd*" *complain about this if I were you. Power to the people. Lots of love, Susan-Bedelia Little."*

"You must have been so confused," Roxy said, trying not to look bewildered herself. It must have been one *seriously* powerful Ever-Youth Charm. It was hard to believe, looking at Sam, that he had first turned eleven years old over *two decades* ago. "Was Susan's note the reason you went and searched my sis— er … Director Humperdinck's office?"

Sam nodded. "That's where we first saw the words *the Missing*: on some top-secret files in there."

"Yeah, look, I know you want to pretend you're adventurers too," Jones said, with a needling glance in Charley's direction, "but the files can't have been all that top secret if they just let you wander in and have a good old nosey."

"We didn't *wander in*," snapped Charley. "It was a pretty cool mission, actually. I mean, obviously we weren't as spectacularly well equipped as you *professionals*, with your party frocks and your super-convincing aliases … but we were smart enough to pick the night of Director Humperdinck's big welcome barbecue, while everyone was distracted."

Now that Roxy thought about it, she remembered the night a little over a month ago when Gretel had stayed out late, and had come back to their bedsit in the small hours of the morning, smelling, unusually, of charcoal smoke. As Roxy already knew, the story Gretel had concocted the next morning – working late as one of the cleaners at a Ministry event – had been yet another lie. But being confronted, now, with new information about her sister's Other Life, that churning, burning feeling was rising up in her stomach again.

"So we found all these files," Sam was going on, "labelled *The Missing*. There was all this information about the kids here, all three hundred and forty-two of us … where we came from … our surnames … our families…" His voice wobbled, and then cracked. "I mean, we didn't actually find my file, or Charley's – there were too many of them – but we haven't had the chance to sneak back in there since."

"Don't think about that stuff, Sam," Charley said, getting to his feet and coming over to give his friend a so-brief-you-could-almost-miss-it pat on one shoulder. "We'll make it back in there one day soon, and then we'll find everything we need to know about you and me. Patience, yeah?"

Sam nodded, but didn't seem able to speak.

"We didn't know," Charley went on, speaking for his friend, "that we'd been in here for all this time. They put us under an Oblivious Charm, we think, to wipe our memories clean. But they can't use a super-strength one because we're just kids. Oblivious Charms are Category Five – the most powerful charms of all – and according to the files we found in the office, Magiscientists have to be super-strict about the correct magic dosage. So they re-enchant us every two weeks. They call it Meditation Club." Charley managed a wry grin. He seemed to be relaxing, just one or two notches, now that this big secret was out in the open. "The rest of the clubs are just to keep us all busy – so we don't question stuff too much, I reckon – but Meditation Club is compulsory."

"Except we've managed to fool them, and skip it. For a whole month!" Sam gave a wobbly grin as he wiped his eyes on his sleeve. "Ever since we worked out what it really––"

He broke off at a sudden sound, coming from the wall just behind his head.

*Tap … tap … tap-tap-tap. Tap. Tap-tap.*

"What the hex is that?" Jones demanded. "Hey, is it your prisoner neighbour?"

Ignoring her, Charley darted over to the wall, crouched down and started to tap in reply. It was evident that the wall was little more than thin plasterboard.

"*That's* your attempt at Morse code?" Jones said, scornfully.

"Oh, and you're the expert, I suppose?" Charley snapped.

"You don't need to be an expert to know you're doing it all wrong." Jones crouched beside him. "What are you trying to say?"

"Uh, how about, *Stop interfering, you absolutely massive pain in the bum*?"

"Funny." Jones sat back on her haunches and gave him a round of sarcastic applause. "Hilarious, in fact."

"Well, just leave me alone." Charley began to tap again. "We really don't need Frankie any more confused than he already is. Or maybe *she*. We're not completely sure which, to be honest—"

"*Frankie?*" Jones and Roxy spoke in unison. They stared at each other, eyes wide in amazement.

"You mean to tell me," Jones jumped to her feet, "That the so-called prisoner on the other side of this wall is called Frankie?"

"Wait – you *know* Frankie?" Sam demanded.

"Well, we know *a* Frankie," Roxy began. "He's Jones's fairy godmother."

"*He's* her fairy god*mother*?"

"Um, well, yes – that's why that whole not-sure-if-they're-a-he-or-a-she thing is sounding quite familiar…"

"Hang on." Jones turned back to the wall.

104

"F-R-A-N-K-I-E," she announced each letter as she rapped it out in Morse code. "T-H-I-S-I-S-J-O-N-E-S."

There was a short silence.

Then there was a massive bang, a brief shower of lavender-coloured sparks, and a large hole was blasted in the plasterboard wall, right where Jones was crouching.

Standing on the other side of it was her fairy godmother.

**8**

"Come through at once!" shrieked Frankie. "It'll close up any moment!"

Jones grabbed Roxy with one hand and Sam with the other, pulling them through the hole with Charley hot on their heels, before it closed up a mere second or two later.

"Awesome stuff, Frankie," Jones said, giving him a quick, fierce hug. "Was that a Blasterrific Charm?"

"Yes, and I shouldn't have done it at all!" Frankie, who was clutching a primrose-yellow silk kimono around himself, wafted away the small cloud of lavender-scented smoke. "I've been strictly prohibited from using magic! That phone –" he jabbed a finger towards a telephone on the nearby wall – "is going to ring any moment with an irritable Magiscientist asking me to explain my... *Told* you!" he finished, as the phone rang and he went to pick it up.

"Yes … yes … that was me… Just an accident, that's all – no damage done… Well, *that's* a bit rude… Yes, I promise…" He slammed the phone down and advanced on Jones, pulling off the matching yellow shower cap he was wearing and using it to swat his goddaughter several times in rapid succession. Despite the kimono, and the bouffant grey curls that had been released by the shower cap, he looked exactly like a ten-year-old boy, and not the three-hundred-and-sixty-four-year-old female fairy he in fact was, all thanks to the extremely powerful Ever-Youth Charm he had accidentally placed on himself several months previously. "What on earth are you doing here?" he yelled. "Is this another of your crazy treasure-hunting missions? Did you learn *nothing* from the last time you went charging about the kingdom sticking your noses into magical mysteries?"

"You mean the time we single-handedly stopped evil Queen Bellissima from *bringing back Diabolical Magic and taking over the world*?" Jones said, pointedly. "'Cos I think that's one magical mystery that we *needed* to stick our noses into."

"Ooooh, and you're Charley." Frankie wasn't even paying attention to Jones any more. He took a hes-itating step towards the tall, handsome figure right behind her, almost looking as if he was about to bob a curtsy, before turning it into a funny little twirl of excitement. "Of course I'd recognize you anywhere. It's been so lovely tap-tap-tapping to you for the last couple of weeks!"

"What do you mean you'd recognize me anywhere?" Charley was staring at Frankie in utter bewilderment (though quite a lot of this, Roxy suspected, was down to the kimono).

"Whoopsie!" Frankie shrieked, turning pink. "Could you just *forget I said that*, dearie? I can't pop an Oblivious Charm on you, unfortunately! Anyway, from what you've told me through the wall, it sounds like you've had enough Oblivious Charms to last a lifetime!" He finished this up with a nervous giggle.

Charley did not join in. He frowned. "Look, could you tell me what you meant by—"

"Fabulous frock, by the way, Roxy!" Frankie changed the subject with about as much subtlety as a rampaging rhinoceros, taking a piece of scratchy blue lace between his fingers to admire it. "It suits you, dear! Who'd have thought: Roxy Humperdinck, all grown up!"

"Humperdinck?" Charley's eyes darted to Roxy. "You mean … like … *Director* Humperdinck? Are you *related* to her, or something?"

"Yes, but it's OK!" Roxy held up both hands, seeing the alarm on his handsome face. "She's my sister, but—"

"Hey!" Charley glared at her. "You lied to us!"

"I didn't lie! I just failed to tell you something. It's different," said Roxy, desperately. "Look, Charley, Sam, I swear ... I'm not, you know, *with her*, or anything!"

"Quite the opposite," Jones added. "Gretel doesn't give two hoots about Roxy. Roxy's a free agent. A lone wolf. No annoying family to weigh *her* down!"

"Oh, but Gretel's not annoying! She's an absolute treasure." Frankie beamed at them all. "She made this place all cosy for me; arranged for my things to be brought from home, even my favourite teapot and biscuit tin! Now, you must be the other chap that's been tap-tapping!" Frankie bustled forward to greet Sam. "Simon? Solomon? Salvador!"

"Um. Sam?" said Sam, looking suddenly doubtful that this was, in fact, his name.

"*Really*? I could have sworn you were a Salvador." (Frankie, Roxy noticed, did not seem to recognize Sam the way she'd recognized Charley.) "But where are my manners? Let me get you all a nice cup of instant hot chocolate and some delicious Cinnamon Snurples. They're a shrunken-giant speciality… Oh, but of course, you know that! You've certainly been here a while!"

While Frankie fussed and flapped over the two boys, guiding them to a chintz-covered armchair and pressing a faintly alarming kitten-patterned biscuit tin into their hands, Roxy gazed around the room, which – this was the first thing she noticed – did not look in the least like a prison cell.

It was just as cavernous as the boys' dorm, with the same high, vaulted ceilings and massive windows, but here the resemblance ended. There were two of the chintzy armchairs at one end, separated by a little coffee table covered with gossip magazines and a small TV. In one corner was a tiny kitchen area, complete with a sink, a kettle, and a sandwich toaster that reminded Roxy of the Snelling's one back in Tent City. Here Frankie was now selecting various sachets of hot chocolate from a kitten-patterned jar that matched the terrible biscuit tin. At the far end of the room was a neatly made-up bed, with pretty white bed sheets and plumped-up pillows in various sorbet shades. Beside it was a bedside table, displaying a little vase of plastic lilies and a collection of porcelain Scottie dogs that trod a very, very fine line between charmingly whimsical and plain old creepy.

"I told you your sister had all my best things

brought from home," Frankie was calling, from the other end of the room, as he stirred the huge teapot full of hot chocolate and selected several mugs from the mug tree. "D'you know, dearies, I'm so comfortable here, I might never leave!"

"Then why did you tell us you were a prisoner?" Charley asked. He seemed to have forgiven Roxy for not mentioning her sister, at least if his relaxed body language was anything to go by.

"Did I, dearie?" Frankie frowned. "Well, that might have been a *teensy* exaggeration when I first got here. But I was feeling pretty cooped-up until they brought my TV."

"For heaven's sake, don't say *TV* too loudly. You might wake Mirror up," said Jones, who had been skulking around the room, rattling the catches on the huge windows and peering at cracks in the stone wall as if she suspected there might be spies peering in from the other side. "Is this a *rubbish chute*?" she added, as a large handle she had just pulled up revealed an absolutely massive and rather chilly hole in the wall.

"Oooooh, I think that's an old dumb waiter, actually," Frankie answered. "From back in the days when the castle was a giant hotel – that's a hotel *for giants*, by the way, not just a really, really large hotel. It became a tourist attraction up here after that silly boy tried to run off with the original owner's golden harp and magic hen. Of course, when Jack and that giant realized what a big news story it had all become, they teamed up and decided to go into business together! After the Compulsory Giant Shrinkage Decrees were passed a couple of hundred years ago, I even thought about coming for a little weekend break up here myself, but the prices were *exorbitant*. That's why I'm making the most of it now! And be careful, that's an antique!" Frankie hurried over and closed the sliding panel over the hole, with a severe glance at Jones. "I was hoping they might even use it to send my meals up from the kitchen, like in the olden days, but they just bring me room service instead. Not that I'm complaining – the food here is fabulous—"

"OK, enough about the accommodation," Jones interrupted. "What exactly *are* you doing up here, Frankie?"

"Well, it just so happens," said Frankie, taking the teapot off a tray and lowering his voice to a dramatic whisper, "that you are looking at SkyZone's brand-new secret weapon!"

"That *teapot*?" Jones asked, incredulously.

"Not the teapot!" Frankie glared at her. "*Me!*"

"But, Frankie, you're a fairy, not a Magiscientist." Roxy, knowing how touchy Frankie could be, was trying very hard to sound less disbelieving than Jones.

"You're quite right, dearie – I'm a fairy, not a Magiscientist." Frankie used the teapot to begin sloshing sickly sweet-smelling cinnamon-scented hot chocolate into the mugs. Above the swirling steam, his eyes – bizarrely still the rather watery eyes of an elderly lady – were twinkling. "But I'm a fairy *who has cast an Ever-Youth Charm that simply won't budge*."

"We get it. You're really, really bad at spells," said Jones. "But how's that meant to help a bunch of elite Magiscientists?"

"I know!" said Charley. "It's because *we're* all under an Ever-Youth Charm that simply won't budge, isn't it?" He and Sam were now both staring at Frankie. "All us kids up here at SkyZone. Is *that* why you're here? To help the Magiscientists reverse the charm?"

"Exactly!" Frankie beamed, passing mugs around and opening the biscuit tin. "It's a funny story, actually. I'd gone to Mortadella's spa, you see, to ask for her help in reversing this dratted charm."

"Mortadella is a good fairy down on the ground," Roxy told Charley and Sam. "She runs this kind of retreat in the Fabulous Forest, for stressed-out witches—

"And her magical skills are second to none!" Frankie interrupted. "Which is why I thought

113

*she'd* be the person to crack my little problem. It was clear, though, from her first few tries, that any reversal attempt was going to make things worse." He gave a little shudder. "I shan't upset you, dears, with some of the terrible things that happened to me when Mortadella attempted an advanced-level charm-repeller. Let's just say that I became more of a ten-year-old boy than ever, most distressingly –" he lowered his voice – "in the *flatulence* department."

"Yeah, well, we all know a few boys that are full of hot air," Jones said, before continuing, smoothly, "So that's when Mortadella thought about sending you to SkyZone? For them to help you, or for you to help them? I mean, did she *know* about all the kids up here?"

"Oh, Mortadella knows *everything*." Frankie was offering round the biscuit tin, glaring at Jones when she took three of the rather misshapen cookies, and shaking it encouragingly at Charley when he only took one. "More, even, than most of the high-ups at the Ministry. So as soon as she realized my Ever-Youth Charm was *that* impenetrable, she contacted the new Director – Gretel – right away, to see if I could be of any help to the SkyZone programme. Because, as it turns out –" he paused for a moment, trying not to look *too* pleased with himself – "I may be the only BOBI in the entire Universe *ever* to have performed an Ever-Youth Charm as unbreakable as the one the Pied Piper placed on the children who went missing."

Roxy finally got it. "They're using you to reverse-engineer the Ever-Youth Charm!" she exclaimed.

"Clever girl!" Frankie raised his mug in a salute. "But then your sister's terribly clever too. This whole reverse-engineering thing was *her* idea. That's the reason she was made the new Director – promoted above Mrs Smith, if the gossip among my new Magiscientist chums is to be believed. In fact, I don't think old Wincey even *knows* about this place," he went on, unable to disguise his pleasure at being in on a secret that was kept even from a Ministry high-up like Mrs Smith – or, as he had known her in the days before the Great Clean-Up, Wincey the Wisteria Fairy. "Can you imagine that? Little old me, Francesca the Flotsam Fairy, more important than—"

"What's *reverse-engineer*?" Sam cut in. He was sitting forward on his chintzy chair, gazing at Frankie as if he was Santa Claus, the tooth fairy and a brand-new puppy all wrapped into one. "And whatever it is, does it mean you're going to be able to lift the Ever-Youth Charm so they'll eventually let us out of here?"

"It just means starting with the end result and trying to work out how you got there," Roxy explained. It's sort of going backwards, in the hope that you can unravel the way something works."

"Exactly, dear!" said Frankie. The Magiscientists seem to think that if they can devise an exspelliment to reverse *my* charm, they might be able to come up with a similar exspelliment to reverse the Piper's! And then the children can be sent home! Well, there'll need to be some special magic worked on their families, of course, so they don't all collapse with shock … but that sort of thing is all being dealt with by the administrators in the Re-Entry department here." He waved a lofty, lavender-scented hand in the general direction of the door to the rest of the castle. "My top Magiscientist colleagues and I are busy working out the *precise exspelliments*. Actually, we're hoping for a huge breakthrough tomorrow night, when the Law of Sevens takes effect."

"Law of Sevens?" Charley's face tensed. "I've heard those words before…"

"Of course you have, dearie! Back in the old days, before the Great Clean-Up, *everyone* knew about the Law of Sevens!" Frankie shot Jones a sour look. "I'm assuming a great magical expert like you knows everything there is to know about it."

"Obviously, me and Roxy know *all* about the Law of Sevens!" Jones fibbed. "But you're the real expert, Frankie! You should be the one to explain it to the boys."

If Frankie had been a peacock instead of a small boy, he would have been strutting right now. "The Law of Sevens," he began, lowering his voice to a dramatic whisper, "is a *natural law* of magic. Law, as in the law of gravity, that is, or the laws of physics, not a law passed by a politician. Now, do you boys remember anything about the Witching Stones?"

Sam shook his head, looking more dejected than ever, but Charley was frowning, on the verge of unearthing another memory.

"Yes, I think I do… They're the stones that all the magic in our kingdom is channelled through, right? Good magic or … whatever the other kind is called…"

"Diabolical Magic," Jones told him, loftily. "Which is kind of relevant to the predicament you've been in for the last two decades. Just saying."

"Are you always such a know-it-all?" Charley asked, raising a dangerously pleasant eyebrow.

"Well, you know –" Jones flashed back an equally dangerous grin –"if a person *does* happen to know it all—"

"Tell us more about the Witching Stones, Frankie," Sam interrupted. "Please?"

"Witching Stones reboot themselves once every seven years, at midnight on the dot, to boost their magical strength for the *next* seven years." Frankie helped himself to another Cinnamon Snurple and snuggled down in his armchair; Roxy could tell he was enjoying this. "So at precisely midnight tomorrow night, *all seven Witching Stones will power down for a fraction of a split second before they reboot with a massive power boost*. The Magiscientists here are hoping to harness this massive power boost for the new trial exspelliment they've developed…"

"Wait – the Law of Sevens means that the Stones *power down*?" Roxy frowned. "Isn't that a bit dangerous? Don't we need them to keep us protected from Diabolica?"

"Oh, don't worry, dear, the powering-down part is *eyeblink*-brief. I believe," Frankie added, proud to show off his new knowledge, "they call it a *nanosecond*."

Just at this moment, the sound of a bell rang out, making Sam jump to his feet.

"That's the end of Club Time! Everyone will be making their way back to the dorms in a minute."

"You can't stay in here!" Frankie shrieked, clasping his kimono around himself in alarm. "My new

Magiscientist colleagues are coming in to wire me up to a DreamOnitor before I go to sleep. I should tell you all about the DreamOnitor sessions, they're ever so interesting..."

"Another time, Frankie, yeah?" Jones was already pulling her kitbag onto her back. She pointed a finger at Charley. "So, Mr I'm-Always-Sneaking-Around-the-Castle-at-Night. Tell me how Roxy and I are going to get safely out of here. Well, it doesn't have to be safely. Unsafely is fine too."

"Um, I think we'd *rather* it was safely, though," Roxy began, "if it's all the same to you..."

"You're leaving?" Sam asked, in a querulous voice.

"Well, we can't stay up here in SkyZone for ever!" Jones told him, briskly but kindly. "We're adventurers, me and Roxy. We *find stuff*. Our mission was to find the Missing. Well, we've found you. Now, obviously, *rescuing you* would be a whole new mission..."

"You haven't found all of us."

It was Charley who had just spoken, though he looked astonished by his words the moment they came out of his mouth.

Not quite as astonished, though, as Frankie, whose face had turned a sickly shade of yellowish-green that was clashing, violently, with his kimono.

"You've remembered?" he gasped.

"Remembered what?" Sam was looking between Charley and Frankie. "Charley, what have you remembered?"

"I'm not sure…" Charley banged his forehead with the heel of his hand in frustration. "There's something … something about someone we left behind…"

"Can't you tell him, Frankie?" Roxy asked, raising her voice as the bell rang a second time. "You seem to know what it is he's struggling to remember."

"Oh, my dears, I can't possibly do that!" Frankie wrung his hands in anguish. "It would be terribly dangerous! A person who has been under an Oblivious Charm should never be suddenly confronted with information about their past. It's a Category Five charm! Even the child-safe version is powerful magic you shouldn't be messing with!"

"But we were OK when we found Susan Little's note. I mean, sure, I vomited for two hours without a break, but once that stopped, I was pretty much fine. Anyway, you aren't *confronting* him! He's already started remembering!" Sam said, desperately. "Isn't that right, Charley?"

"I don't know. I think I am." Charley gazed at Frankie, his chocolate eyes pleading. "Please. Do you know? Did we leave anyone behind in that mountain?

A person who … really mattered to me?"

Frankie was looking pained. "It's too big. It's too risky. I just can't…"

"OK. Enough chit-chat. If you want to find out about this final Missing person you guys clearly left behind – sorry, Frankie, but it's *so obviously* true –" Jones added, as Frankie let out a yelp, "then your best option is to *do something*." She looked directly at Charley, tilting her chin in a challenge. "So. You coming with us, or what?"

"What?" Charley blinked at her.

"Escaping. Getting out of here. I said, didn't I, that our mission was to find the Missing? Well, if there's still one Missing person left, me and Roxy are going to find them, even if you're too scared to join us."

"We *are*?" Roxy squeaked.

Jones pulled, once again, at the handle on the wall. "You think this is an old dumb waiter, right?" she asked Frankie. "So that would mean it would lead all the way down to the kitchens?"

"Well, I think so," Frankie began, "but…"

"And would anyone be in the kitchens at this time of day?" Roxy, who was rapidly cottoning on to Jones's plan, asked the boys. "Any of those kitchen giants you mentioned?"

"No." Charley shook his head. "No food is served

121

after Club Time. The kitchen giants will have finished up for the night by now."

"Then what are we waiting for?" Jones was already clambering into the dumb waiter. "Let's go!"

Charley looked at her, then he turned to Roxy. "What do you think?"

"Me?" Roxy was taken aback. "You're asking *me* what you should do?"

Charley shrugged. He looked, in this moment, very young and very lost. "You seem to know what you're doing," he said. "You seem like a person who has the answers."

"Oh, wow, you're mistaken. I'm absolutely not—"

"You should do it," Sam jumped in. He reached into the biscuit tin, took out a large fistful of Cinnamon Snurples and wrapped them, with slightly trembling fingers, in one of Frankie's lace doilies. "You'll need these," he said, handing them to Charley. "Food for the journey."

Charley turned his gaze from Roxy to Sam. "But what about you?"

"I can't come with you." Sam gave Charley a little push in the direction of the dumb waiter. "One of us has to stay here and cover for the other one. I can probably fool them into thinking you're just in bed with a headache for a day or two. After that, I'll have to get a bit more inventive but I reckon I can get you four, five days of freedom, at least. And anyway, you'll be back by then, right?" he went on, with a wobbly grin. "Let's just hope that if they've managed to lift the Ever-Youth Charm by then, you'll still recognize me."

"Sam…" Charley protested.

"Guys!" Jones rapped on the side of the dumb waiter with frustration. "Come *on*!"

Roxy, flinging off her shyness for what she was pretty sure would only be a moment, grabbed Charley's hand. "Jones is right. Sam's right. Let's go."

Charley seemed to make up his mind, and pulled Sam into a brief hug. "I'll recognize you," he said. "No matter what. And I'll see you in a few days. I promise."

"Doesn't anyone care what *I* think?" shrieked Frankie.

"Another time, Frankie!" Roxy gave Frankie's shoulder a squeeze as she pulled Charley towards the dumb waiter. "You can tell us when we bring Charley back for your charm cure!"

"Decided to join us, then?" Jones asked, as Charley swung himself up into the dumb waiter beside her and then reached a hand back to help Roxy.

"Yeah, well, you know." Charley grinned confidently. "Always happy to help a couple of damsels in distress."

"Oh, you are literally the most obnoxious boy I've ever—"

"Hold on tight," Roxy interrupted, pulling the inside handle so the hole in the wall closed up, and then reaching for the large green **GO** button. "I don't know how fast this thing is going to drop…"

## 9

The dumb waiter did not drop down at all.

It shot upwards.

"Are the kitchens AT THE TOP of the castle?" Jones yelled, toppling sideways and grabbing Charley to stop herself from falling flat on her face (though quickly recovering and making it look like she was trying to stop *him* from falling).

"No! They're right at the bottom, in the old dungeons!" Charley yelled back. "I don't think this goes to the kitchens after all!"

"You don't say!" Jones rolled her eyes. "Roxy, I think you pressed the wrong –" the dumb waiter (if, indeed, it really was a dumb waiter) lurched to a stop – "button," she finished. The first to recover herself, she then hauled open the door from the inside. "Oh. My. Stars," she breathed. "It's only a blooming treasure hoard."

The three of them leaped down from the dumb waiter. The attic room they'd arrived in was filled – from floor to ceiling, from wall to wall – with gleaming, glittering *treasure*. In the moonlight, which shone through the vast skylights above, Roxy could see towering piles of enormous gold coins; wooden chests the size of rubbish skips overspilling with massive rubies and sapphires; and golden household objects, from ornate chairs and tables to…

"The giant's harp!" Roxy breathed, noticing the enormous golden instrument, barely covered by a small dust sheet, over by the treasure room's wooden doors. "From the so-called fairytale!"

"Oh, this is seriously epic," Jones was saying, gazing about the dusty attic at all the precious artefacts of the Cursed Kingdom. Her eyes were dinner plates.

"I never knew there was a hoard like this in the castle!" Charley reached out and touched the smooth side of a massive ruby. "I mean, I knew giants liked treasure, but a stash this size? Oh wow!" he exclaimed, pointing at a golden egg the size of a small minibus, nestling in a corner. "Is that *solid*, d'you think?"

"Jones, no!" Roxy suddenly yelped, as she saw Jones pick up a diamond-studded circlet that could have been a giantess's bangle but was the size of a hula hoop. "We can't take anything. And we can't just linger! The idea was to get *out* of the castle, remember?"

"Fine. I mean, it would make an awesome hula hoop. But ruin all the fun, why don't you?" said Jones, sulkily, putting it down again. She unzipped her kitbag and pulled out the rope she always kept in there. "OK," she went on, jerking her head up at one of the massive, star-filled skylights way above their heads. "I reckon we could find a way to climb up there, and then—"

"Hey, let me out!" came a sudden loud yell from inside the kitbag. "There's objects here – enchanted ones, like me! I sense them all around this place – I've woken up, you see!"

"Sorry," said Roxy, seeing Charley's eyes widen in alarm. She darted to Jones's bag and pulled Mirror out before Jones could zip it away again. "This is our friend Mirror. It's … well, an enchanted mirror."

"Woah." Charley was staring at Mirror. "It *talks*?"

"Oh, it talks. It talks *all the time*. And in rhyme, just to add to the super-fun experience," said Jones, slinging her rope over one shoulder. "Didn't you see these sorts of things all the time, back in the Cursed Kingdom?"

"I … you know, I think I did…" Charley was rather pale. "I *have* seen talking household objects before— Oh! I remember!" He let out a bark of over-excited laughter, thrilled at the sudden memory. "A talking teapot! It used to complain like anything if it was filled with Darjeeling tea instead of Earl Grey!" He reached out a hand, fascinated, and took Mirror from Roxy's. "Is it OK if I have a closer—"

Mirror let out a gasp so loud that it was more of a shriek. "Your Highness! Is it really you? The royal prince! Oh, wowzers!"

"The *what now*?" said Roxy.

"Those jeans are rather scruffy, sire," Mirror added, regaining its composure. "Not very regal trousers."

"Hold on." Jones grabbed Mirror from Charley's hand and held it up herself this time, to reflect Charley's shell-shocked face. "You're saying he's some *royal prince*? *This* guy?"

"Not just *some* prince!" Mirror sounded aston-ished at Jones's ignorance. "Prince Charming, heir to Ariadne's throne!"

"But … he can't be," Roxy interrupted. "Queen Ariadne's son is called Prince Ludovic. He's almost seventeen, and he's kind of short, and he keeps appearing in toothy pictures on the front of gossip magazines…"

"They had *him* to replace the first!" snapped Mirror, furious at being doubted. Then, as it realized that the

128

three of them were staring at it in stunned silence, it let out a little squeak. "He *couldn't* not have known…"

"He's been under a powerful Oblivious Charm." Roxy was the first to find her voice. She took Mirror from Jones, as much to calm herself as to make the enchanted looking glass feel better. "He's only just started remembering a few things about his past."

"Oh, whoops," said Mirror, sheepishly. "Oh, dear. Oh, heck. My bad. I've set things quite asunder. You're not supposed to blurt this stuff. It's quite a massive blunder."

"I'm … a prince," Charley managed to croak. "That's … it's…"

"It's blooming *terrible*, is what it is!" Jones looked furious. "Thanks a *bunch*, Mirror. I mean, as if he needed any more excuses to be pleased with himself. Now he's the heir to an actual throne!"

"Well, jointly with his sister," Mirror said, eagerly. "She's the other royal twin."

"I have a sister?" Charley's words were a rasp now. "A *twin*?"

"He didn't know that, *either*?" groaned Mirror. "Oh, I *really* cannot win!"

Charley grabbed Mirror back from Roxy and looked right into his glass. "Her name is Charmian," he whispered. "Isn't it?"

There was another short silence.

"I think I ought to say no more for now…" Mirror began.

"Oh, come *on*, Mirror! You've blurted out plenty so far," Jones said. "Confirming a blooming *name* is hardly going to make his head explode. And if it does, at least it'll stop him being *so annoying*."

"All right, I'll tell." Mirror sighed. "Yes, Charmian's your sister's name. You don't look very well," it added, nervously.

"I remember…" Charley's words were barely audible. "Months in that mountain with no way out … and then one day, I don't know how, we managed to roll back the stone blocking it … I was getting everyone out, while she … while Charmian was gathering up all the little ones who were too scared … and then just before she scrambled out herself, the stone…" He sat down, suddenly, on the base of the harp. "It must have been a spell that suddenly kicked in, or maybe the Piper knew we were escaping somehow, even though he wasn't even there … but the stone rolled back, trapping her—"

"GUARDS!" came a sudden deafening yell. "ALERT!"

It was the massive golden harp, and it was bellowing at the top of its voice.

# 10

"SOME RANCID KIDS!" the harp bellowed, not at all in the floaty, ethereal tones you'd expect from a magic harp. "COME QUICK AND GRAB THE ROTTERS!"

There was no chance – literally none – that a shrunken giant who was even all the way on the other side of the castle was not going to hear this. The harp's voice was so impossibly loud that it was all Roxy could do, clamping her hands to her ears, to stop her head exploding.

And now an actual siren began to sound, almost as loud as the harp's bellow itself. It seemed that the shrunken giants *had* heard, and now the alarm had been raised all over the castle.

"YEAH, SOUND THE SIREN!" the golden harp roared, nastily. "GET THEM ALL! AND SOMETHING SOMETHING OTTERS!"

Presumably, thought Roxy, having been shut away here with nobody to talk to, perhaps for decades, the horrible harp was having trouble getting its rhymes lined up.

"What are we going to do?" she yelled.

"The skylight's shut!" Jones, her hands over her ears, was craning her neck back to look up. "But if we *can* get up there, do you think you can blast it open with that **aperstatus**-thingy spell?"

"Maybe. If they know we're here, I guess it hardly matters if I do an unauthorized spell now. Can we climb up those coin towers?"

"I don't reckon that'll work!" yelled Jones, after a quick shove of one of the towers, which wobbled so violently that several heavy coins fell off the top and clunked to the floor. "They're way too unstable! We'd get buried."

"OK," Roxy bellowed back, "what if we get up there using the other spell I learned from *Basic Incantations*? If a spell can make a shopping bag fly, it can make something else fly, right?"

"*Awesome!*" whooped Jones. "OK, it has to be something we can all fit on. Even Princey-boy. Is he all right?" she added, jerking her head towards Charley, who, like them, was covering his ears to block out the alarm sound, but was also looking as if he might be violently sick.

"It must be the Oblivious Charm! Remember how Frankie said it could be dangerous to suddenly discover truths about yourself?" Roxy crouched beside Charley. "Charley, we really need you to keep it together…"

Jones was already sprinting across the attic towards the massive golden egg and giving it an experimental shove. "Hollow! That means it'll be light enough to fly. *And* there's room for all three of us on it … all *four* of us, fine!" she snapped at the appalled gasp from Mirror.

Well, Roxy thought, flying out of the castle on a golden egg didn't seem a more spectacularly risky plan than any other… As Jones began rolling the egg towards the skylight, she pulled gently but urgently at Charley's hoodie.

"We're going to try and get out of here."

He stared up at her. "Huh?"

"The guards. They're coming. We have to get away, Charley. Please get up."

"This is no time for nicey-nicey, Roxy!" Jones, purple-faced from exertion, was clambering up onto the egg. "Oi, Princey-boy! Just GET A BLOOMING MOVE ON."

"I hate to say it, but she's right," said Mirror. "We

really have to fly! Who'll find your missing sister if *you're* not going to try?"

"I guess…" Charley took the hand Roxy offered and pulled himself to his feet. He cleared his throat and gave himself a little shake. "Golden egg?" he said, sounding more like himself.

"I'm going to make it fly," Roxy told him, with a lot more certainty than she felt.

"Woah." Charley began to jog towards the egg. "Magic. You're amazing, Roxy. Are you *sure* you're not a witch?"

"Of course—" Roxy was interrupted by a sudden loud hammering at the doors.

"OPEN UP IN THERE!" came a loud voice from outside. It sounded rather like Brian G, the shrunken giant they'd met earlier, but angry rather than insanely chirpy.

Charley held the egg steady at the base as Roxy, her heart hammering, scrambled up to join Jones. She handed over Mirror so that she could reach into her shoulder bag for the Grit, then Jones reached down to pull Charley up to sit behind them.

"Right, now I've absolutely no idea if this is going to work or not," Roxy gasped, "but hang on tight."

"It'll work," said Jones, with all the confidence that Roxy did not feel, and seemingly unperturbed by the fresh volley of banging and shouting – multiple voices by now – from the other side of the doors. "Come on, Roxy," she said, eyes gleaming. "*Let's do this.*"

Roxy clasped the Grit as tight as she could in one shaky hand and took a deep breath, casting her mind back to the second of the two enchantments that had popped up on her phone screen.

"*Your shopping bags are heavy – what a hassle, what a chore. So here's a spell to make them fly, to swoop, to glide, to soar…*"

The Grit, buried deep in her right hand, was instantly warm again.

"***Supplex immobilis iubeo ad vitam statim***," Roxy continued, shakily, only to have her words drowned out by more yelling from outside.

"Magiscientists are on their way! If you do not open this door, it will be opened with magic!" they called.

"Hurry!" Charley begged Roxy. "Please!

"***Facti sunt quis robado aliquid***…" Roxy glanced over her shoulder at Jones. "What should I turn the egg into?" she yelled.

"Aeroplane!" yelled Jones. "No, wait, helicopter! We need to go straight up, not taxi along a runway for take-off!"

There was a sudden flash of magical sparks from the door – clearly the Magiscientists had joined the guards now, and it wasn't going to take them more than a minute to spring the doors open...

"*Helicopter!*" Roxy finished the spell, throwing up her arms with a flourish.

Nothing happened.

"**Helicopterus?**" she tried, desperately, in case making it sound a bit more Latin-y would do the trick.

The egg gave a small, but definite, jolt.

"It's grown wheels!" Jones yelled, above the noise of the alarm and the shouting. She leaned down from her vantage point at one end of the egg. "One at the front, anyway!"

"And two at the back!" Charley added, looking down at his end of the egg. "Way to go, Roxy!"

"But we didn't want *wheels*!" Jones howled. "Wheels aren't going to fly us up through that skylight!"

"I know, I know, it's not quite worked. Hang on, let me try agaaaa-aaah..." Roxy felt the egg lurch, rather violently, forwards. The sudden movement caused Jones's left boot, which – as usual – wasn't fastened properly, to drop off and fall down to the ground.

Charley, perhaps misjudging the height, or his own athletic ability, but *definitely* misjudging the importance of Jones's boot, leaned down to scoop it back up.

And toppled off the back of the egg.

"Charley!" yelled Roxy, as the egg shot forward again, ramming the attic doors.

"Grab my hand!" yelled Jones, turning and leaning precariously off the back of the egg to pull Charley back up. "Just hang on, will you?" she added, to the egg.

The egg rammed the doors a second time, even harder – and this time they burst wide open.

Roxy would never quite know whether the egg had broken it down or if the Magiscientists outside had finally magicked it open – it was hard to tell, given that it seemed to have been blown apart at all kinds of crazy angles. For a moment, she could see a bunch of extremely startled faces as a massive golden egg on wheels came thundering through the splintered doors towards them. There were screams and yells as the guards and Magiscientists dived out of the egg's way. One quick-witted young woman wearing a particularly flowing lab-robe lifted her hand to cast a spell to stop them… But Charley flung Jones's fallen boot at her, knocking her sideways before she could unleash any magic. And by now the egg on wheels was already speeding along the wide stone corridor, lit with large and rather fabulous flaming torches, that led away from the giant's attic.

"Lean to the right!" Roxy managed to gasp, because this seemed the only way to steer the egg around the upcoming corner rather than smashing into the solid stone wall ahead. She leaned, Jones leaned, Charley-holding-on-to-Jones's-hand leaned, and somehow, by the merest whisker, the golden egg lurched leftwards *just* before it hit the wall …

… only to arrive at the very top of a very giant-sized flight of very hard stone steps.

The egg reared upwards for a moment, almost as if it was about to stop, somehow sensing the madness of this descent. But it was only an egg after all, and a very recently enchanted one at that, so common sense was obviously too much to hope for. And in any case, gravity had taken over.

"Hold on to your hollyhocks!" yelled Jones, finally managing to haul Charley all the way up onto the egg's back just before the egg began to bump and rattle its way, at considerable speed, down the massive flight of massive steps.

"I am h-h-holding on!" Roxy yelled back, her voice juddering and lurching all over the place. "H-h-how do y-y-you think we're g-g-g-g-going to stop this th-th-th-thing?"

"Are you crazy?" Jones sounded as if she was enjoying this bone-shaker of a ride way, way too much. "We can't stop this thing until we're safely off the beanstalk!"

"Safely?" gasped Charley. "J-j-just how do you th-think we're ever going to get off here *safely*?"

Roxy might have tried to reply, but she suddenly spied a person running up the stairs towards them.

It was Gretel.

## 11

The Director of SkyZone was heading up the steps with as much urgency as the golden egg was rocketing down them, and only just flattened herself against the wall in time. Instead of knocking her flying, the egg merely brushed past.

Her eyes met Roxy's. Gretel opened her mouth, but she looked too astonished for any actual words to come out.

Meanwhile, the egg was now hurtling through the open doorway at the base of the huge staircase, and careering out into the open air.

The night air was crisp and fresh, and what with the stars and the moonlight, it would all have been breathtakingly lovely if the egg's passengers hadn't been rolling at speed across a gigantic leaf several miles up in the sky. Despite its gigantic size, the amount of leaf ahead of them was getting smaller by the minute, taking them closer and closer to the moment they would rocket right off the edge...

"Jones, I'm serious!" Roxy shouted. "We've got to stop this thing. We can't just drive off the beanstalk!"

"No such word as *can't*!" Jones whooped.

"That's just the rubbish teachers spout when you're struggling with simplifying fractions!" Roxy retorted in exasperation. "I don't think it applies to situations where you're about to plummet to your certain doom!"

"Then do some more magic!" Even Jones was sounding a tiny bit nervous now that the egg wasn't showing any signs of slowing down. "Add a parachute! Make us a safety net! Use that massive brain of yours, for Pete's sake! Think of *something*—"

Jones was interrupted by a sudden noise from beneath them.

It was a cracking, exploding sort of noise that Roxy hoped was coming from Jones's bottom and not from one of the egg's wheels blowing out.

And then the sound came again, louder this time.

She looked down.

"I do not wish to spread alarm –" Mirror's voice was wobbly – "however hard I'm shaking. But one of us should speak the truth – this golden egg is *breaking*!"

This was when a large orange thing jabbed out of the shattering shell.

It was quite unmistakably a beak.

"I think there's a chick in there!" yelled Roxy, shooting a glance over her shoulder to see that Jones and Charley were now almost eyeball-deep in a huge mound of golden-yellow fluff.

"Trust me to be at the bum end!" Jones said, sinking deeper into the fluff-heap.

"That's better than the beak!" Roxy shouted, shifting from side to side to avoid getting nipped by the (very hard) beak that was by now frantically pecking and pecking and pecking…

"Can baby chicks fly as soon as they hatch?" Charley called.

"I think," gasped Roxy, "we're about to find…"

The egg launched itself off the edge of the beanstalk.

The remaining portion of the golden shell fell away to reveal the freshly hatched giant chick. For a moment that seemed to Roxy both brief and endless at the same time, the chick scrabbled its brand-new legs in mid-air, not appearing to have the faintest clue what to do with them.

There was a second moment, this time merely endless, when the chick dropped downwards like a stone.

And then something else happened.

The chick began to fly.

It was wobbly, uncertain flight, yes; the chick was lurching up and sagging back down like a knackered old aeroplane flown through a storm by a pilot that didn't know up from down, yes. But the creature was, at least, flying.

"Good chick!" Roxy gasped, reaching up to pat it on the head as it let out a deafening CHEEP of terror. "Clever chick! You're doing really well! Just … just don't stop, OK?"

"And don't look down!" Mirror gasped. "That's quite unwise! Just take it nice and easy!"

"HOW AWESOME IS THIS?" Jones hooted, her voice only marginally muffled by the yellow fluff that still engulfed her.

"I knew you could do it, Roxy!" added Charley.

"But I didn't *do* it at all, really. I mean, my magic spell didn't make the egg fly, it just gave it wheels! I've still no idea what went wrong … or right … and if it hadn't hatched into Chickie here, we'd be pancakes right now." Roxy's stomach lurched. "And Mirror would be smashed into a hundred thousand pieces."

Mirror let out a horrified gasp. "No s-word, please! My nerves! The stress! I'm feeling proper queasy!"

"Would you just chill out and enjoy the view!"

Jones yelled, peering through a break in the clouds to where the Rexopolis lights glittered far below. "It's awesome! Oh, and we're not calling him Chickie," she added. "That's a *terrible* name."

"Well, what do you suggest we call him?" Roxy demanded.

"How about ... Golden Thunder?" suggested Charley.

"Huh. That's not bad, I suppose." Jones leaned towards where she imagined the chick's ear to be. "How would you like to be called Golden Thunder?"

The chick must have liked the sound of this, because he suddenly reared upwards in an excited manner and let out a volley of deafening cheeps.

"Whoa, whoa, whoa!" Roxy gasped, as soon as Mirror had stopped shrieking. She reached out and made what she hoped were calming strokes of Golden Thunder's soft neck. This was as much for her as for the chick, she realized, because her heart was still racing, and the freezing wind rushing past her ears was reminding her just how far *up* they were. "So how are we going to bring Golden Thunder in to land?"

"Oh, we don't need to worry about that yet," replied Jones. "We've got a long flight until we reach the Deadwoods."

"The Deadwoods?" Roxy echoed.

"Yes. That's where His Royal Pain-in-the-Bumness was when he left his sister behind in the Piper's mountain – isn't that right?" Jones asked Charley.

"Look, could you be a *bit* less flippant?" snapped Charley.

"Because you're a prince?" Jones scoffed. "And you think you can tell us how to talk?"

"Because this is my missing SISTER we're talking about, you complete ignoramus!" Charley yelled. "I mean, how do you think it feels, to suddenly discover that you have a missing twin whose existence you didn't even know about for the last twenty years?"

"All right, all right, mate!" But Jones at least had the decency to sound a little bit sorry. "No need to get your knickers in a twist. Me and Roxy both have our family issues too. Don't we, Rox?"

Roxy might ordinarily have blurted out that actually, even though her own siblings appeared to be in permanent hiding from a vengeful child-eating witch, Charley's terrible tale of a long-missing twin left behind in an evil mountain for two decades was *way, way* worse. But she did not.

For one thing, it was obvious what a terrible time Charley was having right now, coming to terms with the shock about the Charmian he'd been shouting for in his dreams. And for another thing, she was toying with an idea. OK, not an idea, as such. A thread of a shadow of a shade of an idea that had, she realized, been coming to her in bits and pieces – one puzzle piece at a time – ever since she had performed that first spell back at Snelling's Roof Garden.

The Deadwoods, Roxy knew, was the terrifying forest in the far, far east of Illustria, where Han and Gretel had long ago made the mistake of ambling into the cottage belonging to the Gingerbread Witch. Gretel had tricked the witch not once but twice, first using the witch's appalling eyesight to convince her that Han was too scrawny to eat, and second, by talking her into peering into her oven. A quick, brave-as-anything shove from Gretel and the evil witch had been shut inside. Oh, yes. Roxy knew all of this from the fairytale, as well as from her brother and sister's stories. But what she also knew was that *no trace of the witch had ever been found*.

What if the Gingerbread Witch was still there, somewhere, hiding deep in the Deadwoods?

And what if with Roxy's astonishing, new-found ability to perform magic – even if it was, right now, dodgy, wobbly, completely chaotic magic – *what if she could do something to take down the witch once and for all*?

No. *No*. It was crazy. It was absurd. It was unthinkable.

But … Roxy was thinking it.

"Anyway, a bit of appreciation wouldn't go amiss, buddy," Jones was telling the prince. "I mean, there are *other* daring adventures we could go on, you know. Nobody *has* to rescue your sister. Admittedly, it'd be pretty rubbish of us not to even try, now that we think she's been trapped inside a mountain for twenty years…"

"Jones." Roxy saw Charley wince. "Come *on*."

"No, look," began Charley, awkwardly. "I really am grateful for all your help."

"But *I* have not agreed to help!" shrieked Mirror. "I'm not some silent minion! It might be nice for you to ask if I have an opinion!"

"Well, unless that particular opinion is: *Sure, Jones, I'm delighted to join in!* then I'd prefer for you to keep it to yourself," said Jones. She was reaching into her kitbag and pulling out the packet of mini marshmallows. "Anyone else hungry?"

"But don't you know the Deadwoods are as evil as can be?" Mirror's voice lowered to an anguished squeak. "They say the witch resides there still…"

"Do they know where?" Roxy asked, sharply, at exactly the same time as Charley said, "Witch? Which witch?"

"The Gingerbread Witch, of course!" Jones

explained, stickily, through a mouthful of marshmal-low. "I'll bet you heard about her back in the olden days. Nasty piece of work. Lured kids into her ginger-bread cottage and then *actually ate them*, which was charming of her. Roxy's brother and sister fell for the scam, in fact, but they were smart enough to get away."

"Oh, *yeah*…" Charley's face lit up at the thrill of another memory slotting into place. "I do remember something! It was all over the news for weeks – a twin boy and girl who'd gone missing… Wait, that was your *brother and sister*, Roxy? That was *Director Humperdinck*?"

"Uh-huh." Roxy took a large handful of the marshmallows Jones was offering her, in an attempt to seem super-chilled and casual. Her stomach was lurching so much that she had no intention of actually eating them. "Can she *really* still be hiding out in the Deadwoods, though?" she asked Jones, shoving the sweets into her satin bag, alongside the Grit. "Doesn't the fairytale say she was burned to a crisp when Gretel pushed her into the oven?"

"Fairytale!" snorted Jones. "We all know THAT can't have been what really happened. I'll bet the witch managed to magic herself out of the oven somehow. And even if she was catastrophically singed before she managed to do that, you know how this stuff works! I mean, Queen Bellissima was only a puff of smoke, and *she* managed to escape the Diabolical prison and turn herself back into an actual person. OK, a sort-of mirror person. And then get turned into a sort-of vegan muffin, Rox. All thanks to you. Well, *us*."

"You girls…" Charley was shaking his head in a mixture of awe and bewilderment.

"You're all ignoring me!" shrieked Mirror. "You ought to heed my warning but you think I'm just a whinger. I hope to heck *you're* not entrapped by houses made of ginger!"

"And you think the old gingerbread cottage is still there?" Roxy asked, over the delighted CHEEEEP from Golden Thunder (who seemed to enjoy Mirror's rhyming chit-chat a lot more than anyone else). "I mean, that's probably where she'd be, right? Close to home?"

"You ask this stuff like I have all the answers!" said Jones, impatiently. "I may know staggeringly large amounts about the Cursed Kingdom, but even I don't know *everything*."

"Don't worry, *I* certainly don't think you know everything," said Charley, mischievously. "I'm under absolutely no illusions about the amount of knowledge you have stored in your unnaturally small head."

"Hey, at least I've not forgotten I have a twin sister."

"Oh, that's cheap."

"CHEEEEEEEEEEEEEEEEP!" agreed Golden Thunder.

"Better cheap than arrogant," said Jones.

"Better arrogant than small and annoying," said Charley.

"Better small and annoying than…"

Roxy tuned them out, clasping on to Mirror's chilly silver frame for comfort. She had no headspace for the Charley and Jones Show, and not just because it was yet another double act she felt excluded from.

As they flew on, towards the Deadwoods, she needed to keep a clear head. After all, she had to work out how to turn her crazy new thread of a shadow of a shade of an idea into something approaching reality.

## 12

Roxy had been gently dozing on Golden Thunder's soft, warm back for who knew how long when she was woken by a sudden steep falling sensation.

This was because they were falling.

*Fast.*

The giant baby bird – hungry, or exhausted? – seemed to have given up flapping his wings. He was dropping like a stone.

"Don't panic!" Jones was practically shrieking. "It's not *totally* bad news!"

"Are you crazy?" Charley shouted back.

"Crazy *excited*!" Jones yelled even louder. "We're right above the Deadwoods! We're going to land exactly where we were aiming for! Try to flap your wings, GT!" she went on, at the top of her lungs. "I know you're exhausted, but if you could just *try*..."

"CHEEEEEEEEP!" bellowed Golden Thunder, wearily. "CHEEEEEEEEEEEP."

"Of course, and I totally sympathize," said Jones, "but just a *teeny* bit of flapping would be ideal right now."

"It's no good!" gasped Roxy, as she saw, through the silvery moonlight, the long, long line of dark trees, that had once been horizon, looming closer and closer with every passing second. "We're going to crash! Goodbye, Jones! And Charley – it's been so nice knowing you, briefly—"

*CRRRUUUNCH.*

It was incredibly lucky, Roxy managed to think, as Golden Thunder landed on a huge snowdrift, that they were landing on a huge snowdrift.

And – this was a massive unexpected bonus – that the chick seemed to have some kind of giant-baby-bird survival instinct to splay its four legs to spread out the impact.

And, it had to be said, that it was quite so massive and fluffy.

It wasn't that Roxy barely felt the impact – she felt it, sure enough, jarring every bone in her body – but no damage seemed to have been done. She could hear the most colossal, feather-shaking snore, so Golden Thunder must be all right. And she could see that Mirror had not been damaged either.

"You're OK!" she gasped.

"I am," snapped Mirror, "but I shall not forget that as you neared your end, you bade farewell to *Jones and Charley*. Am *I* not your friend?"

"Oh, Mirror, I'm sorry…"

"Perhaps you do not need me as you carry on this quest!" Mirror's voice wobbled.

"Mirror, of course we need you!" Roxy held it close in her shaking arms. "You offer … uh –" she racked her shaken brains – "you offer a *reflective surface* that none of the rest of us can!"

"I *do* reflect things rather well," agreed Mirror, sounding a little perkier. "Dear Roxy, you're the best!"

"Uh, hello? I'm over here," came a muffled voice a few metres to Roxy's left. "A little help…?"

It was Jones. Or rather, it was Jones's legs, which were sticking up out of a separate snowdrift like a couple of spoons in a cup of ice-cream.

"Jones! I'm coming!" Roxy slid down the side of the snoring chick and ran towards the snowdrift.

This was when a shot rang out across the moonlit clearing.

Roxy flung herself face first into the snow.

"Who are you?" came a commanding voice from behind one of the towering pine trees. "Name yourself, or I fire again! And this time, it won't be a warning!"

"I'm Roxy, and this is Jones, and —" out of the corner of one eye, Roxy could see Charley's rather alarmed-looking face peeping out from behind a mound of yellow fluff near Golden Thunder's bottom — "Charley!" she gasped. "We come in peace!"

"I'll be the judge of that!" boomed the voice. "What are you doing in the Deadwoods? Who sent you? Where is your craft?"

"It wasn't exactly a … a craft," squeaked Roxy. "It was … well, *that*." She nodded, nervously, in the direction of Golden Thunder. The chick had by now burrowed so deeply into the snowdrift that the only visible part was the yellow tail-fluff above Charley's head. "It's a giant baby chick, hatched from a giant golden egg. I know it sounds really unlikely, but that's what we flew in on. Well, not so much *flew* as *dropped screaming from the sky*, but…"

"GET THAT SNOW OFF THE POOR MITE AT ONCE!" shrieked the booming voice. "THE POOR SHIVERING WEE CUTIE!"

And a large, lumbering woman appeared from behind the pine tree and hastened towards Golden Thunder's snowdrift.

The woman was dressed in the most extraordinary combination of clothing Roxy had ever seen: tartan knickerbockers, green rubber boots, a fur hat trimmed with what looked like an actual tail and a cloak that might have been made from the rest of the animal. She was not, in fact, carrying a rifle, or a gun of any kind – in large, gloved hands she was holding, instead, a very serious-looking catapult, and there was a pouch around her shoulders that looked heavy with stones. Roxy had mistaken the sound of a stone ricocheting off a pine tree for the sound of a firing gun.

"Come and help me dig!" the woman snapped, starting to shovel at the snowdrift. "There's a defenceless chick shivering under there!"

"There's a defenceless boy shivering *under the chick!*" said Charley, desperately.

"OK, let me just get my friend out first…" Roxy began to dig a shivering Jones out, using a squawking Mirror as a shovel.

"GET OVER HERE AND HELP!" roared the woman.

"All right, all right, keep your incredibly weird hat on." Jones was spitting out snow as she and Roxy scrambled to obey the woman. "Great landing, Princey-pants," she couldn't resist sniggering, as she noticed Charley's squashed head beneath Golden Thunder's massive bottom.

"We'll have you out of there in two shakes," the strange woman was crooning, to the snoozing Golden Thunder.

155

"Even less than two shakes would be ideal," Charley managed to utter, as the girls set to work shovelling snow off the huge chick, Roxy stealing a few glances at the strange woman whenever she could. Not only was she unusually tall and broad, and clad in those extraordinary clothes, but her face was remarkable too. She had ruddy, weather-beaten cheeks, a very large snub nose and the most astonishing eyebrows – great dark tufts above darting eyes – that were almost the same shade as the masses and masses of curly, dark-red hair that spilled out from beneath the hood of a fur cloak.

"Wolfskin," the strange woman said shortly, noticing Roxy's stare. "And no, I don't need the lecture about how bad it is to wear fur, thanks very much."

"I … I wasn't going to—"

"I'm the biggest animal lover you'll ever meet," the woman went on. "But *wolves*… Well, if you don't show a wolf you mean business, you'll end up at the business end of a wolf. That's an expression I've always stood by."

"It's … um … not one I'm familiar with," Roxy said, trying to sound as polite as possible, because what other choice was there, out here hundreds of miles from anywhere, with a catapult-toting, wolfskin-wearing stranger?

"Now, grab on, you under there," the woman told Charley, extending a hand to pull him up while Roxy and Jones hoisted Golden Thunder's bottom out of the way. "You look like you could do with— Oh!" Her wide, weather-beaten face turned the colour of the surrounding snow. "It's … it's *you*."

"It is me," Charley agreed, shaking her newly limp hand as if he did not quite know what to do with it.

"I simply can't believe it." The strange woman was looking at Charley, eyes stretched in shock. "*Prince Charming!*"

"*Charming*?" Jones cackled with laughter. "I love it! I thought Charley must be short for *Charles*, or something normal like that!"

Charley ignored her and grabbed the strange woman's wolfskin coat. "You recognize me from the Cursed Kingdom? Do you know any more about me? *Do you know anything about my sister?*"

The woman gently removed his hands from her coat and turned back to Golden Thunder. Her own hands, Roxy saw, were trembling. "The most important thing right now is to get this chick safely inside. He'll fit in my workshop. Nice secure door, big padlock on it…"

"You're going to lock GT in?" Roxy felt a stab of anxiety.

"Don't be silly," said Jones. "The padlock's not to keep him in. It's to keep wolves *out*. Right?"

"Got it in one," said the woman. "Lovely meal the wolves'd make of him. Especially that pack right behind the white bark pines just there."

Roxy shot a nervous glance over her shoulder, where the woman was nodding, but – thank heavens – the clump of pines was a good fifty metres away. Although actually this didn't make it any better now that she knew the drooling pack was there.

"Come on, then. You'll soon warm up helping me tow him to my workshop."

"How far's your workshop?" Jones wanted to know.

"That way." The woman jerked her head eastwards, towards the just-rising sun "See that barbed wire?"

Now that it was being pointed out, Roxy could see that here, about a hundred metres away in the same direction as the woman's workshop, stood a thick fence of many, many strands of extremely nasty-looking barbed wire.

"That's the demarcation fence for the Forbidden Triangle," said the woman. "Do you know what that is?"

"It's the most dangerous part of the Deadwoods," said Jones, rather quietly. "It's thirty square kilometres' worth of forest that no one has dared to enter for the last twenty years."

"And you three have just landed – *smack-wallop* – inside it. Now, I'm getting the chick out, no matter what." The woman reached down to her belt for a rope so thick that it made Jones's look like a piece of discarded dental floss. "Whether or not you kids come with us … well, that's pretty much up to you."

"Just through the barbed wire to your workshop, you say?" said Roxy, plastering a bright smile on her face to hide her fear. "Well, that's absolutely no problem at all!"

The woman nodded. Then she tied her rope into an ingenious slip knot, looped the loop gently around Golden Thunder's hind legs, and took firm hold of the other end. "We're heading for that gap in the fence, right there." She pointed to a scratchy-looking hole in one of the sections of barbed-wire fence. "Cut it myself trying to get through to rescue you. I'll need to make it bigger for the chick, obviously. Now, stay close. And pull *properly*. This forest will eat up a namby-pamby whingy-whiny pain in the bum faster than you can say…"

"Namby-pamby whingy-whiny pain in the bum?" suggested Jones.

The woman glared at her over Golden Thunder's enormous slumbering bottom.

"I'll be keeping my eye on *you*," she said. "Let's get going."

**13**

By the time they had finally hauled Golden Thunder through the gap in the wire fence, dragged the chick to the woman's huge timber workshop, covered him cosily with dust sheets and then slogged further through a fresh blizzard to the woman's cabin, Roxy and Charley had warmed up so much that they had even broken out into a light sweat.

Jones, however, was still shivering and shuddering in a manner that Roxy was starting to find alarming. It did not help that she had rather rudely rejected Charley's offer of his hoodie. Nor did it help that she was only wearing one boot.

"My friend needs to warm up," Roxy said as they followed the woman through the front door of the small wooden cabin. Without asking permission, she shoved Jones down on the sofa nearest the crackling fireplace and pulled a thick red velvety blanket over her.

"Hot soup coming right up," the strange woman barked, as she closed the door behind them. "Sort her out in a jiffy."

"Oh, wow," shivered Jones, trying to sit up beneath the red blanket. "This p-place is *awesome*."

Which Jones *would* say, thought Roxy, because this cabin was exactly her style: packed to its very rafters with more STUFF than Roxy had ever seen in her life. Even by Jones's standards, it was a mess. There were stacks of paper everywhere, as high as Roxy's shoulders, which looked like they might topple over at any moment and bury any unfortunate passer-by in an avalanche. Nestled between these, heaps of mismatching pottery crockery – plates, mugs, serving bowls – were also piled high on the furniture. The sofa that Jones wasn't sitting on was mostly covered with wonky pottery vases; a busted armchair was laden to collapsing point with vast, brightly daubed pottery platters; and a disused toilet in the far corner – Roxy *really* hoped there was another, *working* toilet somewhere else – was topped with a wobbly tower of what looked like gigantic soup tureens.

"OK, so I have a hobby," the strange woman

snapped, noticing Roxy staring. She stood at the other end of the cabin in a cluttered kitchen-ish area, firing up a counter-top gas-ring and dumping the contents of a family size can of soup into another wonky-looking tureen above the flame. "Pottery relaxes me. Do you have a problem with that?"

"No, no! Is – er – is that what you use your workshop for?"

"Partly," said the woman, shortly, but she didn't add any details. "Are you hungry, or not?"

"Do not accept her offers," Mirror, hidden in the folds of Roxy's lab-robe, suddenly piped up. "Don't be tempted by her food! Dear Roxy, *you* should know this stuff! Don't fear that you'll seem rude!"

"Come on, Mirror. Jones needs to eat."

"Jones *always* needs to eat," said Mirror, pointedly. "I've never met a girl so greedy. Well, go ahead! Ignore me! I just hope your end is speedy."

"Mirror has a point," Charley agreed in a whisper. "How do we know that this woman isn't a witch, planning to eat us for a late-night snack?"

"No chance of that," snorted Jones. Warming up already under the thick velvet blanket, the colour was returning to her cheeks. "No one could digest *you* before bedtime."

"Breakfast, then," retorted Charley. "I bet she'd get

a massive amount of pleasure from shoving your head into a soft-boiled egg…"

"I'm planning nothing of the sort!" snorted the woman, indignantly, from the other side of the cabin. "And I am not a witch! Not to mention the fact that I never eat soft-boiled eggs. Can't bear them. They give me terrible wind, as it happens."

"You heard?" Roxy felt mortified. "My friends didn't mean…"

"Oh, it's no big deal." The woman waved away Roxy's embarrassment with a huge hand. "And you'd have supersonic hearing too, if you'd lived alone out here for years, trying to judge by the sound of the howling each night just how close the wolves are. And by the way – you may as well just bring that magic mirror out from under your coat," she added. "There's no point in hiding it. Where did you get hold of an enchanted object like that? SkyZone? Because I know that's where you've come from. No point in pretending otherwise. And I know *you're* his Royal Highness Prince Charming –" she pointed her stirring spoon at Charley – "but I've absolutely no idea who or what you two girls are. You're not Magiscientists, that's all I'm certain of."

"We're collectors," Jones said, unusually meek. "Of ancient artefacts. Of the Cursed Kingdom."

"Ah. Adventurers, then." It was hardly any surprise, given how accepting she'd been about Golden Thunder and Mirror, that the woman took the mention of the Cursed Kingdom entirely in her stride. "Now, then…" She was bringing over three steaming bowls on a tray. "I hope you like mushroom, tomato, and leek-and-potato?"

"All in *one soup*?" asked Jones, dubiously.

"Well, I do like experimenting with my flavours!" The woman proudly handed a bowl to each of them. She gave an awkward bob as she passed Charley his soup, which Roxy decided was meant to be some kind of a curtsy. "This batch started out as mushroom, then a couple of days after that I tipped in a tin or two of tomato … that wasn't particularly nice, if I'm honest, so I've just added a tin of leek-and-potato, and I really think that's done the trick."

"Sounds, er, mouth-watering," said Charley, politely, giving it a little stir.

"Sounds *eye*-watering, more like," grunted Jones, but she took a spoonful anyway. "Actually, that's not half bad," she announced, mouth full.

"Told you!" The woman beamed, suddenly, and rather shyly. "Of course, you lose a sense of what other people like, when you only cook for yourself for so long. Nobody comes here, you see. It's one of the things about living in the Deadwoods, especially so close to the Forbidden Triangle... Which is why I can't understand what *you* were doing," she went on, "crashing down like that, in such a dangerous area, and in the wee small hours of the morning, too. From my notes –" she picked up a scrappy-looking pad from the arm of the chair she was sitting in – "I first sighted you at three forty-six a.m. That's right at the peak of the highest level of Evil Activity!"

"Evil Activity?" Roxy echoed. "Is that ... um ... some kind of technical measurement?"

"Absolutely!" The woman looked even more enthusiastic about Roxy's question than she had about her soup. "Evil Activity in the Forbidden Triangle begins to creep up towards midnight, before hitting its peak at the stroke of twelve, obviously. It's still in the high-to-moderate zone until at least four fifteen a.m. at this time of year, and then it reduces with the break of dawn. But even the lowest levels of EA in that part of the woods can be catastrophically perilous. There's the risk of wolf-attacks, tree-attacks – some of the pines are particularly vicious – and I'm sure I don't need to tell any of you the dangers of finding yourself face to face with a certain Gingerbread Cottage..."

"Have you seen the cottage?" Roxy blurted out. "Do you know exactly where to find it—"

"So what's going down in the Forbidden Triangle

tonight, then?" Jones interrupted, before the woman could answer Roxy's question. "Thanks to the Law of Sevens, that is. I mean, you must know all about the Law, if you're a Magiscientist."

"How did you know I'm a Magiscientist?" snapped the woman.

"Well, it's kind of obvious, isn't it?" said Jones. "There's that workshop out there where you're clearly doing *something* scientific. You have all this Evil Activity data at your fingertips. You barely blinked an eyelid when we flew in on a giant chick. And, more importantly, you knew we'd come from SkyZone. *If you weren't a Magiscientist, you'd never have known about SkyZone in the first place!*"

"It's a fair point." The woman raised both hands in defeat. "OK. I'm a Magiscientist. Or rather, I was a Magiscientist. One of the very few," she added, proudly, "*non-BOBI* Magiscientists. My name is Susan-Bedelia Little. Magical Drone Engineer, at your service."

"*Susan-Bedelia Little?*" Jones dropped her spoon into her soup bowl. Her startled gaze met Roxy's, and Charley's, before they all stared back at their eccentric host. "You're joking, right?"

"Oh, ha-ha, I get it, very funny," Susan-Bedelia Little said with a scowl. "How can I be called *Little* when I'm so hilariously *not* little? It was the same when I was a girl, and I was six feet tall by the age of nine, and thanks to the red hair and the *stupid* red cape my fashion-challenged mother insisted I wear, everyone began oh-so-side-splittingly calling me *Little Red Riding Hood*..."

"Wait – you were *Little Red Riding Hood*?" Roxy exclaimed.

"You've heard the whole made-up load of drivel, then?" The woman – Susan Little – Little Red Riding Hood – gestured her spoon, furiously. "I *never* went off the path to look for bluebells, all right? I hate flowers, they give me appalling hay fever! *And* I never told that horrible wolf that I was going to my grandmother's cottage! What kind of a mindless idiot would I have been to have advertised my destination to a slavering wild animal? It makes me look incredibly stupid!"

"Hey, I remember you!" Charley exclaimed. "You were all over the news, when I was about four or five! You were the first nine-year-old to survive a wolf attack! I saw you on TV when we were still living in Shiny-Newland, before Mum took over the throne here. I thought you were *awesome*!"

"Oh, well..." Susan Little was blushing. "I don't know that *awesome* is quite accurate."

"I had no idea," Charley went on, "when my friend Sam and I got that message you sent to SkyZone, that

Susan-Bedelia Little was the same person as the Wolf Attack Girl! Not that I remembered Wolf Attack Girl until just now…"

"Wait. You got one of my drone messages?" Susan gasped, sitting forward.

"Messages? You sent more than one?" asked Charley.

"*Loads*, over the years, ever since they threw me out! I expected most of them to be intercepted by the shrunken giants. I just kept hoping one would get through one day! Oh, I'm so happy it finally worked!" Susan clapped her hands like a delighted toddler. "Now, tell me: can you describe the drone you received it on? I'm hoping it was my Model C Turbo, because—"

"Can we discuss the drones another time?" Jones interrupted. "Because me and Roxy knew who you are too, as it happens. We have a letter you wrote to my dad a few years ago. Jimmy Jones? The journalist? Do you remember him?"

"Jimmy? Of *course* I remember Jimmy!" Susan gasped. "I mean, we never actually managed to meet in person – I started to worry our letters were being read by MOOOOOH (that's probably what you know as the Soup Ministry, by the way) and I got spooked… But you saw my letter, you say?" Her eyebrows shot up

168

her face. "And you *cracked my code?*"

"Yeah, no offence, or anything, but it wasn't the *most* secure code we've ever come across," said Jones, kindly. "And we know all about MOOOOOH. Believe me."

"But why would the Ministry have been intercepting your letters?" Roxy wanted to know. "You went pretty quiet after you tried to let the world know about SkyZone. And these days you live on the edge of the Deadwoods, miles from anyone and anything. Surely you can't do much harm all the way out here."

"But that's precisely *why* the Ministry watched me back then, and why they're still watching me now! *Because I'm here.* And I know what's been going on *all the way out here* these past few weeks!" Susan rubbed her eyes in agitation. "I mean, obviously I've watched the Deadwoods for years – that's what my drones are for. Even when I was still working at SkyZone, that was the purpose of my department: to send drones out to the most dangerous parts of the forest to bring back any information they could pick up about the missing princess." She gazed over, bleakly and rather hopelessly, at Charley. "Your sister, sire. Princess Charmian. The Drone team's only goal was to find her. And after I was thrown out of SkyZone, I carried on trying. How could I stop, when I knew the truth?

It's been my life's purpose ever since. Well, that, and perfecting my French onion, cream-of-chicken and watercress soup recipe. But obviously the Charmian thing always came first."

"I'm so grateful." Charley sounded, in this moment, more regal than he had ever sounded to Roxy before. "I can't thank you enough, Ms Little, for everything you've been doing."

"Call me Susan, Your Highness, please." She let out a long sigh. "We carried on sending out drones all over the forest after the rest of the children were found, but especially to the Forbidden Triangle. We knew that Charmian had been left behind in the Piper's mountain, and it was always thought the mountain must have been in the Triangle. But I never expected the drones to actually find the mountain *itself*. There must be at least a dozen super-powerful camouflage enchantments on it, to keep it that well hidden. The point of my drones, mostly, was to pick up Whisperings…"

"Whisperings?" Jones's eyes were alight. "What are they?"

Roxy already knew she wasn't going to like Susan's answer.

"The evil in the Deadwoods likes to –" Susan was obviously trying to find the right word – "*communicate* amongst itself. The tree branches; the leaves; the pathways – they're *talking* to each other, all the time. It happens everywhere in the Deadwoods, but it's most intense inside the Forbidden Triangle. I designed the very first drone that was able to pick up the sound of the Whisperings," Susan Little added, proudly. "And I've refined that model over the years, working all on my own out here. I've perfected a drone that's so sensitive it can pick up even the softest whisper from a single pine needle. *That's* how I first knew you were coming in to land – my instruments were going berserk, what with the news of intruders spreading all across the forest. They've been pretty active for weeks, now, but your arrival sent them off the charts."

Roxy had been right: she didn't like this answer. The thought that evil *pine needles* had been watching them crash-land… She shuddered. Clearly it wasn't only the wolf packs they had to fear.

Charley shuffled to the edge of his chair, hunched over his knees. His eyes were fixed on Susan's face. "You say these Whisperings have been worse for a few weeks. Since when, exactly?"

"Ah, now that I can tell you!" Susan lumbered to her feet and went to grab a curled, rather soup-spattered exercise book from near the stovetop. She flicked through it, and then stabbed a finger on a page.

"January the fifteenth!"

"Six weeks ago." Charley looked over at Roxy and Jones. "That's when my dreams started."

"You think," asked Roxy, cautiously, "that your dreams are linked to something that was happening in the Deadwoods?"

"Yes." Charley's face was white. "I think it's to do with my sister... I think she was trying to *communicate with me.*"

"Don't be ridiculous!" snorted Jones, though without much conviction. "That couldn't possibly happen. Could it, Susan?"

"Weeeeeeell ... it's not *impossible...*" Susan mused. "They are *twins*, after all. And actually, there's some excellent Magiscientific data on the ways twins can communicate – well beyond the brainwaves of the rest of us."

"Do you think Charmian was trying to tell me something?" Charley asked Susan urgently. "Do you think ... I don't know ... maybe she's escaped?"

"Maybe ... I don't know! I don't *know* anything!" Susan let out an actual howl of frustration. "I'm just an engineer. I can't understand *what* the evil spirits are saying. But the Ministry has people who can translate – experts in all the old languages from back in the days of the Cursed Kingdom. So I've been emailing and emailing these past few weeks, warning them that they need to listen to some of my audio files, letting them know that I can send them anything they need, but that *somebody* has to listen to them. To listen to *me*! The Witching Stones are going to power down *tonight*, only –" she glanced at the clock on the wall, it was a little past five a.m. – "nineteen hours from now! There'll be this one nanosecond, you see, when *all* the Stones' power will be out – *totally* out. If any *Diabolical* power is strong enough to fill that nanosecond…" Susan shuddered. "I think that's what the Whisperings are about. I think there's excitement about what's going to happen tonight, when the Law of Sevens occurs."

"The Law of Sevens! So it's a real thing, then?" Jones asked. "Not just some superstition, or conspiracy theory?"

"Of course it's real!" Susan looked offended. "Some of my most esteemed Magiscientist colleagues proved it several years ago in a series of exspelliments. There really *is* a quantifiable increase in the strength of atmospheric magic, for just a few minutes, at the stroke of midnight once every seven years. In fact, one of these increases was seized as a moment for Decent-Magic practitioners to weaken Diabolical Magic, exactly twenty-one years ago tonight. If it can be done that way around – good magic seizing control over bad magic – there's no reason why it can't happen the other way."

"And you think that something evil inside the Deadwoods is planning something massive for tonight, precisely because of the Law of Sevens?" Roxy asked.

"All I know is that the Whisperings are on the rise," murmured Susan. "But does anyone at MOOOOOH want to open their great cloth-ears and pay attention to me? No, they do not."

"OK, that does it." Charley got to his feet and strode towards the door. "We have to go back into the Forbidden Triangle."

"Did you not *just hear*," Jones said, incredulously, "what Susan said? Whisperings. Evil Activity." She followed him, blocking the door before he could reach for the handle. "Does any of that sound *welcoming* to you?"

"No." Charley shook his head. "But whether or not my sister was communicating with me, we have to try and find her. Before midnight. If something *really* evil is going to happen in the forest ... tonight could be our last chance to go after her," he managed to finish, softly.

*And it could be my last chance to find the Gingerbread Cottage,* Roxy thought.

"I agree with Charley," she said.

"Oh, well, if everyone's up for some serious adventure, there's no way *I'm* missing out!" said Jones. "You'll be joining us too, Susan?"

"In the Forbidden Triangle?" Susan croaked. "*Tonight?*"

"Or how about right now?" Jones added. "No time like the present, right? And it's almost daylight, so your precious EA level will be lower. I reckon we swoop over the area on Golden Thunder, treat him like a *massive drone*, and then when we see something worth investigating, take him in to land. Or plummet. Or whatever."

"We could really use you," Roxy added, seeing Susan's expression start to change from one of horror to one of nervous excitement. It was a feeling she knew only too well herself. It was like lightning in a bottle: you had to trap it, fast, before sensible things like doubts or reservations started to kick in. "You're really familiar with the woods…" She stopped herself before she blurted out, *and maybe you even know the location of the Gingerbread Cottage*.

"It *could* work, I suppose." Susan's eyes were shining. "We should give the chick another hour to rest while we get packed. We'll need my maps, my best binoculars, a couple of flasks of lovely hot soup…"

"I kind of think we should leave the soup," Roxy

175

said, hastily. "The last thing we want is to spill anything hot on poor Golden—"

She stopped. She could hear something outside.

It was the sound of a helicopter.

## 14

"Stay here, all of you," barked Susan, striding to the front door. She gave Charley a hasty curtsy before shoving both him and Jones out of the way. "Don't let yourselves be seen!"

Charley yanked Jones and Roxy down behind the sofa.

"Manhandle me again," Jones hissed, "and you're *toast*."

"Well, forgive me for looking out for my team-mates!" Charley hissed back.

"I'm not your mate, mate! Team or otherwise!"

"Is there *anything* you won't pick a fight about...?"

"Who do you think is in the helicopter?" Roxy managed to interrupt the by-now-familiar Charley and Jones Show. It was starting to get right up her nose. "I thought Susan said nobody ever comes out here."

The helicopter had landed now, and someone was pounding on the door. Susan opened it, letting in the most colossal draught of air from the helicopter propellers.

"Just lift me up," Mirror said, excitedly, "and I will peep and tell you who is here!"

Roxy had to admit, that was a smart idea. Carefully, she inched Mirror up over the edge of the sofa so that it was facing the door.

"It's *Mrs Smith!*" Mirror whispered. "And several **SMOGs**! With laser guns, I fear!"

"What are you doing all the way out here?" Susan was shouting over the helicopter din. She stepped outside and pulled the door shut behind her. "I've been emailing your people for weeks!" Her furious voice continued to carry through the door. "And nobody even had the courtesy to reply!"

Jones jumped up from behind the sofa.

"You silly child!" hissed Mirror. "That woman said to *hide away from sight!*"

"When we know it's the Ministry? Even if they haven't come 'cos they've tracked us down, we can't just sit here and let them find us! Think of the *mahoosive* trouble we'll be in," Jones added, cunningly, knowing this was how to get Roxy to do what she wanted, and looking startled when she realized that

178

Roxy was already on her feet and heading for the window at the back of the cabin.

"We can't let them stop our mission." Roxy was hauling the window open. "Come *on*."

"That's my girl!" whooped Jones, following her, pausing only to grab the red velvet blanket from the sofa.

"Oh, my – what are you stealing *now*?" gasped Mirror. "It simply isn't right!"

"Give it a rest, glassy," said Jones. "This is so obviously Little Red Riding Hood's cape, and it's not stealing, it's *collecting important historical artefacts*."

Charley, who hadn't taken much persuasion to get on board with the idea, was helping Roxy scramble out of the window. "Wow," he gasped, as the icy air hit him, "it's cold out here…"

"… I've been trying to tell MOOOOOH this stuff for weeks –" Susan's voice was floating through the chilly dawn – "and now you want to take me in for *questioning*…"

"Don't be dramatic, Ms Little." This was a voice that Roxy recognized as Mrs Smith's: pleasant enough, but with a chilly undertone that suggested she would Put Up With No Nonsense. "You're not being taken in for questioning – nothing of the sort! We simply want to talk through everything you've sent us, to try to get a sense of the data…"

"Pig poo!" snorted Susan. "I can give you every piece of data right here, right now – I don't need to come back to Rexopolis with you!"

"I'm afraid you do," came the Ministry official's calm voice. "Now, please stop this fuss and come to the helicopter…"

"I do not like her tone of voice," hissed Mirror. "It gives a nasty feeling!"

"And we'll need the key to your workshop," Mrs Smith went on. "That outbuilding through the trees – I assume that's where you keep all your instruments, your equipment?"

"Golden Thunder!" hissed Jones, staring at Charley and Roxy in panic as they all pressed themselves against the back of the cabin, uncertain where to run. "We have to get him out!"

"No!" A note of panic had crept into Susan's voice too. "You can't go into my workshop! It's out of bounds. It's—" She broke off.

At that moment, almost as if he knew exactly what was going on outside the cosy, warm workshop, Golden Thunder let out a sudden, rafters-shaking CHEEEEEEP!

"What on *earth*…?" Mrs Smith could be heard to gasp in the silence that followed, before the second, even more deafening CHEEEEEEP.

"It's coming from the workshop!" yelled a **SMOG**, and the children could hear the sound of running.

"*Down!*" Jones pulled Roxy down with one hand and Charley with the other, so that all three of them were screened by an old chopping block. A moment later, a herd of **SMOGs** jogged past the back of the cabin towards the workshop.

"We have to get GT out," Roxy hissed, desperately, "before they get to him!"

"I think it's too late for that!" Charley said, as the unmistakable sound of splintering timber filled the dawn air.

Golden Thunder had grown, even in the last hour. The chick was no longer merely huge: he was *enormous*. He was flapping his wings in a panic, and bringing the entire workshop crashing to the ground around him.

"Agent Ford, Agent Carter," yelled the lead **SMOG**, above the sound of tumbling planks, "contain that … er … well, whatever that creature is!"

"Sir, I believe it's an absolutely gigantic fluffy chick, sir!"

"Nobody likes a smarty-pants, Agent Jefferson!" snapped the lead **SMOG**. "Contain it *at once*, will you?"

"Sir, yes, sir!" The agent raised an Instant Paralysis Laser and pointed it at Golden Thunder.

"No!" Jones yelled, leaping up from behind the chopping block. And she plunged a hand into Roxy's shoulder bag to grab the Grit.

"**Aperstatus Hexaflor!**" she shouted, and Roxy winced, waiting for the inevitable flash of light and shower of sparks – because presumably this was Jones's plan – that would distract the **SMOGs** long enough for Golden Thunder to take to the skies.

There was no light-flash. There was no spark-shower.

But, thanks to Jones's outburst, there were now several **SMOGs** staring right at them.

"Uh-oh," said Jones, dropping the Grit back into Roxy's bag. "OK. Plan B. *Run*."

If Jones's Plan B was to draw the agents' focus from Golden Thunder, it was even worse than Plan A. Bright-white IPL flares began to shower down around the children as they raced towards the cover of the trees.

"What *are* those?" Charley gasped.

"Laser beams! Don't let them hit you!" yelled Jones. "You'll be instantly paralysed!"

"CHEEEEEEEEEP!" came a cry from above, and Roxy looked up to see – with a surge of joy – that Golden Thunder had made it into the air.

"Get to the fence, guys, and they'll never follow us in!" Jones shouted. "Show-off!" she added, as Charley overtook her. "Come *on*, Roxy!"

"I'm going as fast as I can!" Roxy gasped, aware that she would always have been by far the slowest runner of the three even if she hadn't been wearing ridiculous heeled party shoes. It was almost impossible to see Jones and Charley on the other side of the fence now, under the dazzling hail of laser beams, but she could tell from their waving arms that they were frantic with frustration at her slowness. "Go on ahead, you two!"

Above the forest, Golden Thunder was flying free now, swooping in a huge circle as he dodged the laser beams, cheeping as loudly as his lungs would let him.

"Stop right there!" the chief **SMOG** was yelling, though whether at the giant chick or at the three children, it was impossible to tell. "Do not go through that fence! Young woman in the unflattering pale-blue ballgown, I repeat: *Do not go through that fence!*"

Roxy came to a halt at the barbed wire, and Charley and Jones began to haul her through by the arms.

"You're blooming stuck!" yelled Jones.

"I think it's her dress!" Charley panted, frantically trying to unhook some of the frothy blue lace from the barbed wire. "I can't get this off!"

"Stupid lace!" screeched Jones, ducking swiftly as a laser-beam passed millimetres from her cheek.

"Well, yeah, it was kind of a bad fashion choice

for a dangerous mission…" Charley was having little success with the fabric.

"I didn't choose it!" Roxy said. "Jones did." But nobody heard her under the sudden ear-splitting CHEEEEEP! from above. Golden Thunder could no longer see them, now that they were hidden by the cover of the overhanging trees, Roxy realized, and he was starting to panic.

"Any minute now, one of us will be petrified by one of those beams!" Jones yelled, ducking again.

"Then you two go on," begged Roxy, still held fast. "Leave me behind." Defeated and miserable, a searing petty jealousy crept into her voice. "It's not like you actually need me, anyway."

"We're not leaving you," said Charley, though – Roxy noticed – he didn't try to argue about whether or not she was needed. Perhaps it was all the mayhem around them. Or perhaps he was just being diplomatic. "I think … I think I'm almost there," he added, wrestling with a particularly stubborn flounce.

"Well, get a blooming MOVE ON!" Jones yelled. "They're getting closer!"

"*Help*, then, rather than just nagging!" Charley bellowed back. "*Do* something!"

"Permit me to deploy myself," Mirror shouted above all the noise, "and use me for protection! I'll bounce those laser beams away! I'm great at redirection!"

"*This is your final warning!*" screamed the **SMOG** captain. His team had all stopped, clearly not prepared to get any closer to the Forbidden Triangle. They continued to take aim, and now that they were standing still, they were firing much more accurately. There was no chance their lasers wouldn't reach their mark. "*If you do not stop and identify yourselves, we will be forced to treat you as hostiles!*"

"I beg you!" shrieked Mirror. "I can be of use! I'd really love to matter! I'll win you time to get away! Don't fret, I shall not—"

Jones grabbed Mirror from Roxy and held it over Roxy's head just as a laser beam headed straight for her.

Mirror shattered into a thousand pieces.

The laser beam had bounced off the glass and rebounded straight back towards the **SMOG** who had fired it, striking him smack in the chest. He toppled to the floor of the clearing and remained motionless. Just for a moment, as the other **SMOGs** stared at their felled colleague, the firing stopped. This was the moment that Charley pulled Roxy free.

Dragging their friend between them, the prince and the artefact-hunter ran deep into the forest.

## 15

"… bet we'd already *be* at the blooming mountain if you hadn't insisted on leading the way for the last three hours," Jones was saying to Charley.

They were picking their way through a particularly dense clump of trees, deep into the Forbidden Triangle; whatever dim light there was this far into the forest had long since begun to fade. They had been walking for hours, and night was drawing in.

"Right. Because those dozen super-powerful Camouflage Enchantments Susan told us about would make this mountain so *incredibly easy to find*." Charley's voice was stuffed to the brim with scorn. He didn't even bother to look back at Jones, scurrying along behind him. "And you're not one to talk. You led the way for well over three hours yourself, and I don't exactly recall you making a huge success of it. I just wish Sam was with me right now, instead of you! *There's* a person who understands teamwork! All you've done is criticize and blame."

"You'd be sunk without me, pal. At least I had the idea to strew mini marshmallows on the ground, so we could find our way back to the fence!" retorted Jones.

"Yeah, which would have worked if we hadn't run out of mini marshmallows after fifty metres, because you *ate most of them on the flight here!*" said Charley.

"Well, I don't see you coming up with any better ideas…"

Jones and Charley had been going back and forth like this for *hours* – ever since they had made it through the fence, in fact – and neither of them seemed to have noticed that Roxy was not speaking to them.

Jones was the one she was *properly* furious with – after all, it was Jones who was responsible for Mirror shattering – but she was feeling pretty angry with Charley, too. He had actually had the nerve to *defend* Jones when Roxy had accused her of being responsible for Mirror's death – actually had the nerve to point out that Mirror had only been an inanimate object, so technically it wasn't possible for it to *die*.

"It *wasn't* inanimate," Roxy mumbled to herself

now, feeling her eyes sting with tears all over again, and using the back of her freezing hand to shove them away. "It was my friend. It actually *cared* about me, which is more than anyone else on this whole stupid planet."

"Are you getting upset about Mirror *again*?" Jones had caught the sound of Roxy's voice. "Look, I've already told you how absolutely awful I feel about that. I really, really do." Her own voice wobbled, for a fraction of a second, but just as Roxy thought maybe this was going to lead to Jones shedding a tear of her own, she got hold of herself, cleared her throat and spoke normally again. "But it was you or Mirror, kiddo. I had no choice. Surely that makes sense?"

"She's not wrong for once, Roxy!" Charley called over one shoulder. "That laser beam was heading right for your head."

"Oh, I'm not wrong for *once*?" Jones snorted. "That's generous."

"Well, I like to keep up morale amongst my troops."

"For the last time, we are not *your* troops!"

"Maybe, but the last time I checked, I was the only royalty around here, so…"

If Roxy had been thinking straight, she might have given them the benefit of the doubt and concluded that all this banter was just their way of covering up the fact that they were absolutely terrified. After all, dusk was rapidly descending, and it was hard not to worry that all they were doing was wandering further and further into the Forbidden Triangle, with no way of knowing where they were going or how to get out. It was hard not to worry about the whisperings of the trees all around them, which were getting louder and louder as the sky grew darker. It was hard not to worry about everything Susan Little had said about the wolves, and about the imminent danger from the Law of Sevens coming to bear at midnight.

But even if all these worries *were* the reason for the Charley and Jones Show, Roxy was past caring. Because poor, shattered Mirror was lying, all alone, on the other side of the demarcation fence, and Jones was the one that had made that happen.

Roxy had never felt so completely alone in her whole entire life.

"… anyway, give Roxy a break," Charley was saying now, from up ahead. "She seemed to really care about that mirror."

"Hey, I cared about it too, buddy!" said Jones. "I mean, it was incredibly irritating, don't get me wrong, but I wouldn't have wished for it to actually … *shatter.*"

Roxy winced.

"Well, I think we should be more worried about

poor old Golden Thunder," Charley said. "Mirror's gone, which is sad, but Golden Thunder's still alive, and he could be in terrible danger."

"*Great* morale-boosting," said Jones, sarcastically. "Anyway, I reckon GT will be just fine. I reckon he's up above the trees right now, watching over us!"

"Oh, you *reckon*?" Charley could sound even more sarcastic than Jones, when he really tried. "Then that *must* be true. Because you're never wrong about anything. Ever…"

Which was the moment when Roxy realized the Grit was gone.

She had reached into her satin shoulder bag to feel for it, starting desperately to wonder if there was *anything else* she could try to turn into a flying object just so she could get away from ALL THE BICKERING. The bag's lining was sticky from the tiny handful of mini marshmallows that she'd been too angry and upset to volunteer for Jones's pointless marshmallow-scattering earlier. And the marshmallows were still there, all four or five of them.

But the Grit was not.

Roxy rummaged again, delving into the little inner pocket where it had been carefully stowed.

Still no Grit.

Back when they were hiding outside Susan's cabin,

back when Jones had grabbed the Grit out of Roxy's bag and then dropped it back inside it again …

… Jones had missed the bag.

Roxy felt as if the floor had opened up beneath her, and she was falling and falling without anything to stop her.

Finding the Gingerbread Cottage was always going to have been a long shot. It was obviously an even longer shot that the Gingerbread Witch would have been there. It was the longest shot to end all long shots from now until the end of time that she, Roxy Humperdinck, would have been able to summon enough magic to defeat the Gingerbread Witch.

But without the Grit, everything went from being improbable to simply impossible.

"Guys." She looked up. Jones and Charley – still bickering, of course – were much further ahead. *"Guys!"*

"… only hope this twin sister of yours has a *massively* different personality…"

That was it.

That was *it*.

Roxy spun on her heel and walked in the opposite direction.

By the time she regretted it – by the time she had cooled off, and realized that being alone in the

Forbidden Triangle, as night fell, was a VERY, VERY BAD IDEA – it was too late.

It had only been fifteen, maybe twenty seconds, but Charley and Jones had already vanished.

"Jones! Charley!" she called. Though she did not know why she was bothering; they hadn't even noticed she had gone, or they'd have stopped and waited for her. "Charley! Jones!"

There was no reply. What there was, instead, was another sound entirely.

The howl of a wolf.

It was blood-curdling, bone-chilling, and in that moment, as the sound reverberated off the pine trees, Roxy could not imagine a more terrifying noise in the entire world.

She realized, only a moment later, that she was wrong; there *was*, in fact, another noise that was way, way more terrifying.

*The howls of an entire pack of wolves.*

Roxy began to run, stumbling her way over tree roots to get as far away from the howling wolf pack as her jelly-legs would carry her. But the howls seemed to be growing louder with every step she took, whichever direction she ran. And there was a new problem now – the tree roots underfoot were growing gnarlier and more numerous, almost as if they were joining forces with the wolves to try to trip her up. *The evil in the Deadwoods likes to communicate amongst itself,* Susan Little had warned. *The tree branches; the leaves; the pathways – they're all talking to each other, all the time…* What had Susan called it, this creepy phenomenon? The Whisperings?

*Thiswaythiswaythiswaythiswaythisway…*

Roxy was pretty sure the whispering was coming from the trees. Which made perfect sense when she considered that Susan had specifically used the term to describe the Evil Activity that went on here in the Forbidden Triangle. Well, she was just going to ignore it, go with her own instinct to escape the howling of the wolves…

*Takethispathtakethispath* … came the whisper of a hundred thousand perfectly synchronized pine needles above her head as she ran. *Fastasyoucanfastasyoucan…*

"Shut up!" Roxy yelled, now almost completely out of breath, and realizing a moment later that yelling was only going to give the wolves more chance of tracking her. "I won't do what you say," she gasped, lowering her voice, "so you can just…"

*… orthewolveswillgetyougetyougetyougetyou…*

"Not listening," Roxy declared, pointlessly, dimly aware now that her feet were thudding along *exactly* the forest path that the trees seemed to want her to go down. In fact – and she *really* did not want to believe this – it seemed like the actual paths themselves were merging into one, shape-shifting before her very eyes into one single path, with no way of diverging off it, as if the paths were just as much a part of the Evil Activity as the trees all around. "I'm not letting you take me to the wolves," she managed to say – suddenly aware that this must be what the forest was trying to do. "I've magicked wheels onto a golden egg… I've reached the top of a giant's beanstalk and flown hundreds of miles from home… I've lost a good friend tonight, who died to save me… Believe me, *you've met your match…*"

The path she was running along came to a sudden end. And she realized that the Whisperings were not leading her towards the wolves after all. They had led her, instead, to a wide, circular glade.

A glade with a gingerbread cottage right in the middle of it.

Roxy caught her breath. Even in the dusk, she could see that the little cottage had crooked gingerbread walls, candy-cane window frames, and glass made from boiled sweets. The roof tiles were slabs of thick fudge, the little picket fence bordering the cottage was made of neat sticks of golden-yellow cinder toffee, and giant mint humbugs had been sunk into the ground to form a crazy-paving path that led to a pretty little gingerbread door.

The door was opening.

*Go inside*, whispered the trees all around. *Goinside insideinside...*

Roxy's heart was hammering. Her mouth was dry. But this was what she had wanted. This was the moment she had been hoping for. She walked quickly towards the cottage.

As she drew closer, she could smell the gingerbread: sweet, sticky and spicy. Close up, it looked so irresistibly shiny that she could not help reaching out a hand to touch it. But touching it was not enough – her hand had pulled off a big, delicious wedge before she could stop it, and she was shoving it into her hungry mouth even as she walked through the door ... and felt it close smartly shut behind her.

Dropping the hunk of gingerbread, Roxy turned and grabbed the candy-cane handle, and pulled.

"It's no good," said a voice behind her. "It's never going to open!"

Roxy spun round, arms raised, chin high, all ready to face the Gingerbread Witch even if she was armed with literally nothing more than four mini marshmallows and a pointless shoulder bag that she could – what? – throw at her? But it wasn't the

Gingerbread Witch who had spoken.

It was Gretel, crouched inside a large cage at the other end of the cottage. She was white-faced and wild-eyed and open-mouthed.

"*Roxy?*" she gasped.

"Gretel!" Roxy ran to the cage and pulled, frantically, at the iron bars of the cage door. "What are you *doing* here?"

"I could ask the same of you!" Her sister stared out at her. "Do you have *any* idea of the danger you're in, Roxy Rebecca Reignbeau Humperdinck?"

Roxy ignored the telling-off, and pulled the bars even harder. "Is there a lock? A key?"

"It's locked *with magic*, Roxy. There's no getting out of it."

"OK, but … well, look, it turns out, Gretel – and I don't want you to freak out about this – but I can do a teensy bit of mag—"

Roxy was interrupted by a whimper from the back of the cage.

There was another person there, she now saw, huddled beneath a tattered blanket.

"It's all right, Your Highness," Gretel said, turning to pat the long, matted dark hair that peeked out over the top of the blanket. "There's no need to be scared. It's not the witch. It's –" she glared at Roxy

– "it's my little sister, actually."

"Highness? Wait – do you mean…?" Despite how terrifyingly bad this situation was, Roxy felt a little bit like jumping for joy. "The missing princess is *here*?"

Gretel nodded. "She escaped from the mountain almost six weeks ago – can you believe she chiselled at a crack in the rock *every single day* for twenty years, until there was a hole big enough for her to crawl out? Luckily the Piper had left a magically regenerating food supply in the mountain, for all the kids he thought he was going to keep holed up there, but it sounds like it was mostly bread, tuna and tinned mandarins— Hey!" She frowned, reality overtaking her apparent admiration for Princess Charmian's two decades of tunnelling her way out of a rockface fuelled only by tuna sandwiches and canned fruit. "How do *you* know about the missing princess?"

"I met Prince Charming at SkyZone. And before I get the whole lecture about how I should never have been there in the first place," Roxy added, quickly, "just consider that if I hadn't gone up there, I'd never be here right now, rescuing you."

Gretel let out a wild, rather hysterical laugh. "You think you're on a *rescue mission*? This is the *Gingerbread Witch's* cottage, Roxy! People don't escape from here!"

"*You* did, once! And Han."

"Yes, and that's exactly why the witch won't make the same mistake a second time. Look, Roxy..." Gretel gripped the bars of the cage so tightly that her knuckles turned white. "The best thing you can do right now is get out of here as fast as you can. The witch said she would be back by nightfall, and it's been pretty dark out there for hours. She'll show up any minute!"

"Yeah, I'm not leaving." Roxy was looking around the rest of the cottage for anything she could use to break the cage open. It wasn't promising. There was an ancient-looking steel bucket in one corner, with an equally ancient mop sticking out of it. There was a wooden pan rack on one gingerbread wall, where a couple of large, very tarnished saucepans were hanging. And in the middle of the back wall was a large, black range oven.

As Roxy took a couple of steps closer to the oven, she saw the heat coming off it.

"You're going to leave this cottage," Gretel was saying, "and you're going to run as fast as you can, all the way out of the Deadwoods, and—"

"STOP TELLING ME WHAT TO DO!"

"Roxy, this is my job, OK? This is my *world*. And I am very, *very* good at what I do..."

"Oh, really? Then how come you managed to get

yourself captured by the Gingerbread Witch?" Roxy stamped her foot in desperate frustration.

"Because I was stupid. I let my guard down. And she's more determined than ever to … to get rid of me." Gretel looked, for a moment, like the frightened little girl she must have once been, inside this very cottage. "There's going to be this moment, at exactly midnight tonight, when the good magic that protects Illustria will blank out, just for a fraction of a second. If the witch is ready, in that moment, to perform the most powerful curse that has ever existed, her own power will grow so vast and so quickly that in a few moments more, Diabolical Magic will have knocked out every trace of good magic that exists in the world."

"But what has that got to do with you?" Roxy asked, stupidly.

"The most powerful curse that has ever existed is the Vengeance Curse." Gretel was talking very fast now. "It's a horrible spell, Roxy – one that gives a sudden jolt of toxic strength to anyone that enacts it. And the greater the lust for revenge, the greater that jolt. I'm the one the witch has been waiting to entrap again all these years. I'm the one she wants revenge on. So, if she kills me at exactly midnight tonight…"

"How very kind of you to explain it all to your sister," came a voice from the cottage door. "That's saved me repeating myself. Full marks to Gretel Humperdinck!"

Roxy whipped round. All right, she had no Grit, and *absolutely no plan whatsoever*. But she was ready, at least, to look the Gingerbread Witch in the eye.

"And, of course, I'm always happy to welcome a visiting child. After all, that's what the gingerbread is there for!" said the witch.

Or, to be more accurate, *Mrs Smith*.

"*Sominem Cadaverus*," Mrs Smith said sharply, and pointed a fingertip at the cage.

Roxy saw a shower of purple sparks – and then knew nothing more.

## 16

Roxy did not know how many hours had passed. All she knew was that the Knockout Spell was wearing off, and that she was waking with the mother of all headaches. She also felt sick. The kind of sick feeling that comes after a shock so nasty you can barely comprehend that it's happening.

*Mrs Smith is the Gingerbread Witch. The Gingerbread Witch is Mrs Smith.* Repeating it to herself did not make it seem any more real. She had known Mrs Smith was intimidating; she had known she was responsible for maintaining the Ministry's grip on the country and making sure its citizens remained oblivious to their magical history. She could never possibly have imagined, though, the terrifying truth about who Mrs Smith *really* was.

Roxy opened one painful eye to see that Gretel and

Princess Charmian were flat on the floor of the cage, still out cold from the very same Knockout Spell. She could also see that she, Roxy, was now inside the cage beside them.

This, she was pretty sure Jones would have said if she were here, was a massive, *massive* bummer.

On the other side of the cage door, Mrs Smith was fussing, unhurriedly, with the stove, fiddling with a rusty dial near the oven doors. She was singing, under her breath, what sounded like a nursery rhyme.

*"Girls and boys come out to play, the moon does shine as bright as day…"*

Cold panic swept over Roxy. Was this actually happening? How had Mrs Smith fooled everyone? Not just herself and Jones – even though, Roxy grimly thought, if she *did* make it out of here without getting eaten, she was going to have some *serious* bones to pick – no, no, bad choice of phrase – some *serious words* with that know-it-all Jones, who hadn't *known* or even merely suspected this! But maybe she was being unfair. Mrs Smith had somehow pulled the wool over Gretel's eyes. And had, presumably, fooled every top-brass high-up at the Ministry, including Minister Splendid himself! How in the name of Diabolica had she done it? Jones was right: she had obviously not been burned away in that oven. She must have used her magic to escape it after all. Roxy's head was buzzing with the difficulty of making sense of it all, buzzing as loudly as…

No. What she was hearing, right now, was a *real* buzzing sound, from outside her head, not inside it.

It was a motorbike engine.

Mrs Smith turned to open the front door. Roxy shut her eyes again, tight, and tried to control that feeling of panic.

"You took your time," Mrs Smith was saying to whoever had just arrived. "And you look," she added, crisply, "perfectly ridiculous."

Roxy opened her eyes a fraction; she could see a motorbike's headlights being switched off, leaving the clearing bathed in soft moonlight.

"Hey, this is a big night," came a man's voice. It sounded irritated. "What's wrong with dressing up a bit? You could stand to make a bit more of an effort yourself!"

Mrs Smith didn't reply, but her silence evidently spoke volumes. When the mystery man spoke next, he sounded more uncomfortable.

"Well, anyway, what does it matter what I look like, so long as it's mission accomplished?"

"It is not *mission accomplished*," said Mrs Smith, icily. Her voice became clearer as she came back into the cottage, and returned to the stove. "And it won't *be* mission accomplished until midnight strikes and I finish off Hansel and Gretel Humperdinck once and for all."

*Wait*, Roxy just had time to think, *did she say Hansel*?

But the mystery man was speaking again. "Shall I carry Han inside, then?" he called through the front door.

*Oh, no, no, no, no, no*, Roxy thought. *Not Han, too*. Not another person she loved…

"Yes, right away. The Vengeance Curse will only reach maximum strength if it strikes both of them at once. Put him down over here by the stove," Mrs Smith added, as the man came in after her. "There's no need to put him in the cage. It's already ten to midnight. Time to get started."

The man carrying a lifeless-looking Han through the gingerbread door was – Roxy stifled her gasp, only just in time – Solomon Sax, H-Bomb and the Missiles' drummer.

He was wearing ludicrous flowing robes, in the same purple and red as the outfit he had been wearing on Snelling's rooftop, and even without the addition of the wooden pipe now tucked under one arm, it was pretty clear that he was not just a rock-band drummer. He was the Pied Piper.

The fury that surged through Roxy was helpful: her blurry, fuzzy, shell-shocked mind felt as if it had snapped quite suddenly into sharp focus. All these years, Sax had been a part of the Missiles – travelled the world with Han, written mega-hit songs alongside him, acted as his friend and mentor. And all along, he'd been hiding his secret identity, biding his time, along with Mrs Smith, until … well, until what? Until this moment and this place – midnight in this cottage – when Mrs Smith could wreak double revenge on the two children who had once thwarted her, and use the power generated to seize Diabolical control of the kingdom.

Moving as slowly and carefully as possible to avoid being noticed, Roxy dipped a hand into her evening bag again. After all, perhaps she'd made a mistake, perhaps the Grit really was still inside… But no, there was nothing in there but those leftover mini marshmallows.

"Remind me again –" the Pied Piper was puffing, now, as he lugged the lifeless Han towards the stove, dropped him heavily on the striped mint-humbug floor tiles (Roxy flinched) and then perched for a rest on a barley-sugar window ledge – "do we need them dead *by* midnight, or at the stroke of it?"

"The very last stroke," said Mrs Smith. "If we enact

the Vengeance Curse in that exact window, enough Dark Magic will be released to strengthen Diabolica ten thousandfold, wiping out the power of Decent Magic in an instant."

The Pied Piper grinned, eyes glittering. Then, perhaps overcome with excitement, he took his wooden pipe from under his arm and started to play.

"It almost makes me happy," Mrs Smith was saying to herself, opening the stove doors again, "that those two foul children turned me to little more than a lump of smouldering charcoal, making it necessary for me to find another body to inhabit: that stupid old Wisteria fairy – a respectable Ministry official. Now, when Decent Magic is entirely wiped out, my official Ministry status will make it so much easier for me to round up every single child in this entire kingdom. Those three hundred-odd little wretches my friend the Piper here procured for me all those years ago – and then *lost*, lest we forget – will be nothing to the numbers I will be able to get my teeth into now. Isn't that exciting, child?"

It was only now that Roxy realized: Mrs Smith was not talking to herself. She was talking to her.

"I can tell you're awake, little girl," Mrs Smith went on. She came over to the cage, leaned down and peered inside. Her eyes were very bright and her teeth seemed very sharp. "I wonder, would you tell me just one thing? Did my False Memory Enchantment work on you, back in the Decontamination Zone that day? Or should I have listened to the instinct that told me it hadn't?"

Roxy swallowed, hard, and struggled to sit up. "It didn't work," she said, looking right into Mrs Smith's watery blue eyes, behind her pebble-thick glasses. Now that she knew who the elderly fairy really was, she could see nothing but evil in them. It was remarkable that she hadn't seen it before. "And *this* isn't going to work either," she went on, her heart hammering. She clenched her fists. "You're not going to kill my brother and sister. You're not going to unleash whatever evil you think you're going to unleash. I'm … I'm going to stop you!"

"*Are* you?" Mrs Smith's eyes widened. "Well! That really *would* be remarkable, dear! Might I ask how you plan to do it?"

Roxy opened her mouth, but no words came out.

"Fascinating," said Mrs Smith, after a moment. "Now, perhaps you'll excuse me? I have a Vengeance Curse to prepare, and only –" she glanced down at her watch, through her thick glasses – "six and a half minutes before the first stroke of midnight."

"Not another Humperdinck?" the Pied Piper said,

taking his pipe momentarily away from his lips.

"Yes, another Humperdinck," said Mrs Smith, straightening up. "We'll deal with her and the princess after we've finished off the others. I'll certainly be hungry by then."

The Piper began to play his pipe again. This tune was different: a sultry, mellifluous melody. Roxy could tell it would soon lull her into the kind of hypnotic state that Charley and the other missing children had succumbed to.

*Unless she could stop it.*

She reached a shaking hand into the evening bag and pulled out the last two mini marshmallows. Stuffed into her ears, they might be enough to ward off the terrible power of the Piper's music, at least for long enough for her to think up that plan – that plan that she so, so desperately needed...

She looked out of the cage. The Gingerbread Witch was still busy at her stove, which had now started to pump out thick wafts of gingerbread-scented steam, as if preparing itself for something. And that *something*, Roxy hardly dared to think, was likely to involve her sister and brother.

Without the Grit, without her ability to perform even the smallest act of magic, there was no way she could stop this.

It was weird, then, that her fingertips were suddenly warm.

It was exactly the same sensation, Roxy realized, as she usually felt when she was actually *holding* the Grit. That same honeyed heat coursing through her hands from the tips of her fingers. That same feeling that if she just uttered the words of a magic spell, something extraordinary would happen.

She did not know exactly what she was expecting when she raised her right hand, pointed it at the cage door and whispered the words of the spell she had already used to split a hole in a water mattress and open up the lift to SkyZone.

Nothing at all happened to the cage door.

But the pale-yellow sparks that shot wildly out of Roxy's fingertips in all directions blasted a pretty massive hole in the iron bars *and* the gingerbread wall behind her.

## 17

Gingerbread debris, shattered candy canes and chunks of cinder toffee flew through the air.

Roxy had a moment to take in the scene – a shocked Mrs Smith turning from her stove and the Piper covering his face to fend off a ricocheting lump of cinder toffee – and to think to herself as she stared in amazement at her tingling hands, *Well, this is weird*, before something even more astonishing happened.

From way above the cottage came the sound of a deafening CHEEEEEEEP!

Golden Thunder.

Roxy jumped out of the freshly blasted hole in the wall and peered up to see the immensely heartening sight of the colossal chick circling the clearing in the moonlight.

"There's Roxy!" yelled a familiar voice – Charley's

– from somewhere near Golden Thunder's fluffy head. "She's coming out of the cottage!"

"I have eyes, you know!" This was Jones. Roxy had no idea if Jones and Charley had found Golden Thunder or if Golden Thunder had found Jones and Charley, but either way, the two of them were right there above her, riding on Golden Thunder's back. "Roxy!" Jones shouted down. "Are you clear of the cottage?"

"Yes! Wait – no!" Something in her friend's voice suggested that Jones needed her to be clear of the cottage so that she could *do something*. Something dangerous. Possibly something massively destructive. "I have to get my sister and brother out! Your sister too, Charley! She's here!"

Before Charley could answer, Jones yelled, "Yeah, look, if you could maybe get on with that soon-ish, Roxy? We're operating on a schedule here!"

"You don't know the half of it!" Roxy reached back through the hole in the gingerbread wall and grabbed Princess Charmian by the wrists, pulling her out into the clearing with a strength she didn't know she had. "Whatever you're about to do, Jones, you have to wait!"

She didn't hear Jones's reply as she darted back into the cage a second time, ready to pull Gretel clear.

But it was too late. Mrs Smith had recovered from her shock and was already opening the cage door from the other side. The Pied Piper was pulling out the unconscious Gretel to join her twin brother right beside the steaming-hot stove.

"Ignore this!" Mrs Smith snapped, as the Piper glanced anxiously upwards, perhaps waiting for another deafening bird call, or maybe concerned that he might get hit by more treacherous lumps of toffee. "In three minutes' time, we'll destroy them all with nothing more than a sideways glance!"

"All right!" The Piper let Gretel drop to the floor beside Han. "Do you need me to play?"

"Do what you like!" Mrs Smith looked as if she would quite happily destroy *him* with a sideways glance. She raised both hands over Han and Gretel's motionless bodies and began to chant. "*Sweet revenge shall soon be mine, send a shiver up my spine...*"

"Stop!" Roxy raised her own hands, stepping out of the open cage. But then she felt a powerful strike of magic hit her hard in the stomach. She doubled up, falling to the floor.

"I'll handle her," said the Piper, who had cast the spell that had knocked Roxy down. "You concentrate on the curse."

"*Hear my call for retribution,*" Mrs Smith continued,

as the Piper strode towards Roxy. "*Bring about this swift solution…*"

The Piper placed his hand on Roxy's head; she felt warmth course through his fingertips, ready to perform whatever spell would take her out of action entirely.

"*Children*," he spat, with loathing in his voice. "No better than rats, if you ask me."

Gasping for breath, Roxy lifted her own hand. She could hardly fit him with wheels, or open him like a door, but she did know one more spell that might do the job. The trouble was, of course, that it was quite clearly a Diabolical spell … but this was not the time to be choosy.

"**Sominem Cadaverus!**" she shouted, and could hardly believe her eyes when the very same kind of purple sparks that Mrs Smith had used to knock her out earlier shot from her own fingertips and sent the Piper flying backwards.

He hit the floor and did not move.

"Impressively fast learning, child," snapped Mrs Smith, distracted for a moment from her curse. "You have quite the knack for Diabolical Magic. A pity you won't be around much longer to enjoy it."

"Stop. Stop right now!" commanded Roxy fiercely. Mrs Smith placed her hands on the double oven doors.

The stove seemed to be growing, if that was possible, as soon as the witch touched it: expanding upwards and outwards.

"One step closer," said Mrs Smith, pointing a gnarled finger directly at Roxy's head, "and you won't even live to see your brother and sister's end."

Roxy felt panic rise in her chest: she might be displaying an impressive (and truly *astonishing*) ability to perform magic without the Grit, but she knew she would never be fast enough to block a Diabolical spell from a proper witch. "You are *not* putting them into that oven, Mrs Smith!"

"Too blooming right she's not!" said Jones, striding through the hole in the back of the cottage. She was holding a test tube high in front of her. "Fresh from a SkyZone laboratory!" she declared. "A highly experimental – oh, and massively dangerous, by the way – *time-altering serum!*"

"There is no such thing!" snarled Mrs Smith.

"Oh?" Jones arched an eyebrow; she had always been a way better liar than Roxy. "Are you absolutely certain of that, Witchy-poo? Because trust me, whatever evil you're planning at the stroke of midnight," she went on, "it will all be mucked up the moment I chuck the contents of this test tube into the air! Time will freeze like ice, and you'll never be able to take advantage of the Law of Sevens to … well, what the heck *are* you trying to do?"

"She's planning to use a Vengeance Curse to kill Han and Gretel!" Roxy gasped. "And use the power boost to take over the world, and, basically, eat every child in it!"

"Well, *that's* not happening," said Jones, uncorking the test tube. "I always knew you were totally bogus," she added, to Mrs Smith. "I mean, those *glasses*, for instance. Who needs *glasses* as thick as those, unless they're as blind as the Gingerbread Witch? Right, Roxy? You noticed the *glasses* too, didn't you?"

Roxy could not understand why Jones was putting quite so much emphasis on the word *glasses*.

Then she got it.

Just as an infuriated Mrs Smith raised her hands to complete the Vengeance Curse, Jones flung the test tube and knocked the glasses right off her face.

A moment later Jones herself was sprawling, sent flying by whatever hasty spell Mrs Smith had cast at her, but the witch's glasses were on the floor beside her. Across the other side of the cottage, the Gingerbread Witch was now crouched down, scrabbling blindly about for her glasses.

*She could not see without them.*

Feeling like she was inside a dream, Roxy darted

forwards and opened the massive double doors of the ever-growing oven. Then she stepped back, raised both hands and pushed the Gingerbread Witch inside.

There was no time to cover her ears against the outraged scream. She slammed the oven doors and then turned to haul Jones to her feet. Then she grabbed Han by the armpits and, using every last ounce of her strength, began to pull him towards the cottage door.

"Come on!" she gasped, and Jones followed, panting, as she pulled Gretel behind her.

"We're out!" Jones yelled into the night as soon as she'd cleared the doorway. "Deploy missile!"

"*Missile?*" Roxy said.

"Yeah, you don't think we're going to let her magic her way out of that oven again, do you?" said Jones. "I'd get down if I were you," she added, as there came an almighty CHEEEEEEEP! from above, and then an even more almighty CRASH! as Golden Thunder unleashed a massive golden egg from his – or actually, come to think of it, *her* – nether regions, and dropped it right on top of the Gingerbread Cottage.

**18**

**SIX WEEKS LATER.**

The guard outside the Palace gates stared at Jones and Roxy for so long that Roxy was starting to worry he wouldn't let them in after all.

"I knew it," Jones hissed, under her breath, "I *knew* you shouldn't have worn that awful old hoodie…"

"Jones, there was no way I was wearing that scratchy ballgown again!"

"Well, I can't blame you for that – I mean, you did nearly end up a witch's midnight feast while wearing it, so I accept it holds bad memories – but couldn't you have at least tried to glam yourself up? I mean, look at me!" Jones put a hand on her hip: she was wearing her usual outfit of brown baggy trousers, brown leather jacket and aubergine-coloured trilby atop newly dyed banana-yellow hair, and she looked, as ever, absolutely fabulous. "Now that we know you're a witch, Roxy, you need to start thinking about your look."

"I'm not a witch!" Roxy hoped the Palace guard wasn't paying attention to this, but luckily he seemed too awestruck simply to be in their presence. "And I'm only part … whatever it is I am," she went on, in a low voice. "Gretel thinks it must be from my mum's side of the family. It's definitely not our dad's side, or Gretel and Han would have magic skills too. We won't know for sure *what* I am until the test results come back from SkyZone."

"Well, my money's still on witch," Jones said cheerfully. "Or maybe a sprite. Definitely not a gnome. I don't even think gnomes can do magic…"

"Miss Humperdinck," the guard finally managed to say. "Miss Jones …"

"It's *Ms* Jones," said Jones. "Actually."

"… it's such an honour to meet you both. The saviours of the royal twins!" The guard looked as if he might cry. "Everyone here at the Palace – everyone in the *kingdom* – owes you the most enormous debt …"

"You're welcome." Jones waved a lofty hand. "It was a breeze, really. The hardest part was putting up with His Most Obnoxious Royal Highness's personality."

"… and please, allow me to welcome you to Queen Ariadne's Palace! If you just make your way through this door –" the gate guard took a huge bunch of silver keys off his waistband and used four of them to open up the locks on the gilded entrance gates – "I believe some *very special guides* will be waiting on the other side, to take you to Her Majesty's throne room."

"Thanks so much," said Roxy, feeling a bit awkward as the guard gave a series of little bows, and then relieved as he locked up the Palace gates behind them. "Is everyone going to be like this, Jones?" she whispered, clutching her stomach, queasily, and wishing they hadn't stopped off at Mrs Kettleman's Traditional Custarde Doughnut Emporium for a (double) portion of Twice-Glazed Caramels.

"Just enjoy it, kiddo!" Jones, undaunted and not remotely nauseous, was practically bouncing through the archway that led to the Palace courtyard. "It's not every day you get taken to Queen Ariadne's throne room by special gui— Oh, no," she groaned. "Oh, *nooooooo*."

Waiting for them in the courtyard was Charley. He had a grin on his handsome face and he looked, Roxy was relieved to see, exactly the same as he had the last time she'd seen him, when they'd flown safely in to land at SkyZone the night they'd destroyed the Gingerbread Cottage. She knew that the Ever-Youth Charm had been successfully lifted – Frankie had phoned them last week, triumphant, the very day he'd returned to his flat – but she hadn't been exactly sure, until this moment, if it had actually been *reversed*.

"Charley!" Roxy, at least, was delighted to see him. She ran the last few steps and flung her arms around the prince.

He hugged her back. "It's so good to see you! And dear, sweet Jones –" he grinned – "it's an absolute pleasure to welcome you to my *massive* Royal Palace." He waved an arm around the enormous courtyard: a dazzling vista of white marble and gleaming gold, with serried ranks of footmen, gorgeously attired in purple and gold livery and bowing low at the sight of the prince. "Whaddya think?"

"It's all right." Jones shrugged. "I mean, if you *like* living in a totally stuck-up place like this, where I'll bet you get yelled at for so much as bouncing a ball."

"Well, that depends." Charley put his head on one side, musing. "You'd probably get into a *bit* of trouble if you bounced a ball in one of the eighteen separate treasure rooms – all three of my own personal crowns are kept there, by the way. And you might get yelled at, I suppose, if you bounced a ball in the cinema, or the recording studio, or the burger bar ..."

Jones let out an involuntary whimper.

". . . but you'd *probably* be OK if you bounced a ball

in the basketball court," Charley went on, with relish, "or the all-weather cricket pitch, or one of the tennis courts that Sam and I are going to play on for *hours* as soon as he's allowed out of SkyZone—"

"Is there seriously a recording studio?" Roxy asked, mainly to prevent Jones from self-combusting with fury.

"Yup." Charley lowered his voice. "My younger brother wanted one put in, apparently, when he was thinking of releasing an album a couple of years ago." He and Roxy exchanged a look that indicated they both knew what a colossally bad idea Prince Ludovic's proposed album would have been. "He's spent quite a bit of time in it, actually, since Charmian and I came home. I think he's planning to sulk until Mum and her councillors have worked out which of us should be first in line to the throne— Oh, hey, talking of Charmian," he finished, as a new figure approached them. "What's up, sis?"

Princess Charmian, bouncing towards them, looked more like Charley than Roxy had thought possible. All these weeks after escaping from the mountain, her skin was beginning to lose the ashen-grey colour it had been the night Roxy had first met her; the only difference in the twins' thick black hair was that hers swept rather wildly down past her shoulders instead of simply flopping over her forehead like her brother's did. She was wearing ripped jeans and a black T-shirt with the words *Keep Calm and Carry On (Being a Princess)* in jagged white letters, and she was expertly carrying two huge ice-cream cones in each hand.

"Raspberry ripple for you," she said, handing one to Charley. "Double chocolate-chip, I thought, for you –" this one was for Roxy, handed to her with a fond smile and a little wink – "and for you and me, Jones, I asked the Palace ice-cream chef to magic up that special maple-and-bacon flavour you were talking about for the entire flight from the Deadwoods!" She handed over the second largest of the four cones to Jones and then grinned around at all of them as she began to enjoy the largest cone of all. It was overflowing with golden-coloured ice-cream, complete with sticky-looking bacon bits.

"You have an actual ice-cream *chef*?" hooted Jones.

"Oh, well, we have a whole ice-cream parlour, actually," Charmian said, tapping her cone against the others the way a grown-up would chink glasses. "Here's to us!"

"Here's to us," Roxy agreed, tucking into her own cone. "And it's so good to see you both settled in!"

"Yeah, but not for long, dude," said Charmian. "As

soon as Mum lets us, Charley and I are planning to head off to see the world. I mean, after all those years we both spent shut away, the very last thing either of us wants is to spend the rest of our lives trapped in a royal life. Ooooh, you guys should *join us*—"

"Whoa, hang on a moment!" Charley interrupted, looking alarmed. "Join us on our world tour? Roxy I could handle, but *Jones*…?"

"My dears!" There came a sudden shriek from a middle-aged lady who was crossing the courtyard to join them. She was wearing a peach-coloured towelling tracksuit, a fuchsia sweatband round her grey curls and bright-white trainers. "I had no idea you were coming to the Palace this early! I'd have rescheduled my morning jog!"

Roxy blinked; the voice was familiar, but the person it was coming from was so different … except … she wasn't … not really…

"*Frankie?*" she said.

"Who else, dearie?" Giving off clouds of lavender perfume, Frankie kissed first Roxy and then Jones heartily on each cheek. "Wonderful to see you both!"

"You, too, Frankie. Um … why are you jogging round the Palace courtyard?" asked Roxy.

"Oh, well, it's the strangest thing, dearies! Obviously, we didn't manage to *reverse* the Ever-Youth

Charm so much as *unlock* it, so at least Charley and all those other poor kiddies will have already started growing older again, day by day, just as they should. In my own case, there was rather a stark reversal. The Magiscientists said it was probably because the original Ever-Youth Charm I'd put on myself was extraordinarily wonky!" Frankie looked bizarrely proud of herself. "Anyway, I'm quite rapidly heading back to being my three hundred and sixty-four-year-old self. The Magiscientists think it's a matter of a few weeks now. I mean, I'm two hundred and fifty-six already!" She jogged on the spot, beaming widely. "So really, I'm just trying to make the most of my youth while I can."

"I think," said Jones, "Roxy was asking why you were jogging *here*. In the Palace."

"Didn't you know?" Frankie stopped jogging and peered out at them, breathlessly, from beneath her sweatband. "I have an office here now. Queen Ariadne has given me a job! I'm Deputy Assistant Chief of…" She clapped a hand over her mouth. "Oh, giddy-giddy-goodness me! It's still top secret! I mustn't say a word!"

"Too right," came a voice from right behind them. It was Gretel, who had appeared through a nearby doorway and sidled around one of the saluting footmen without any of them noticing. "Hello, you two," she said, rather severely, to Roxy and Jones. "Welcome to the Palace. I *still* can't believe you're actually being awarded the *Royal Medal of Supreme Courage and Fortitude*." She folded her arms, in her scarlet leather coat, and glared at them both. "Nobody should be rewarded for the sort of wild, reckless behaviour you've been exhibiting."

"Yeah, but you know –" Jones grinned up at her – "saving the world, and all that?"

"Hmmmm." Gretel pressed her lips together to prevent a smile. "Well, the ceremony isn't for another twenty minutes, so I suppose there's time for you to look around a bit. Your Highnesses –" she bowed her head at Charmian, and then at Charley, to Jones's immense irritation – "is there anything you'd particularly like the girls to see while they're here?"

"The basketball court," Charmian began, "and the cinema—"

"Actually, I think they might like a tour of the stables," Charley interrupted, giving his sister a meaningful look.

"Oh, of *course* you think that!" Jones rolled her eyes. "Because we're *girls* we have to be into *ponies*, right? I bet you think we want to plait their manes and put ribbons in their tails, and—"

225

"Ugh, no, who wants to do any of *those* things?" said Charmian impatiently. "My brother thought you might like to see Golden Thunder's corner of the stable block! Well, not so much a corner, really, as an entire wing…"

"GT!" Jones gasped. "Come on, Roxy! Get a move on, Frankie!"

"Hang on a sec." Gretel caught Roxy's sleeve before she could follow. "I haven't had a chance to ask. Are you ready for this?" she said, in a low voice.

"The ceremony, you mean?" Roxy squirmed. "I don't know. It's nice, and everything, but … it's all a bit embarrassing, to be honest."

"Yeah, well, just so you know, there will be a lot of people watching." Gretel ticked them off on her fingers. "Minister Splendid – I think he's going to give a speech, unfortunately – and of course the Queen, and Charley, and Princess Charmian… Nobody's seen Prince Ludovic for the last week, he seems to be having a bit of a tantrum… Oh, and Han will be there. He just flew in last night."

"You didn't tell me he was coming! *Again*." Roxy said, pointedly.

"Well, there was no point, really. I mean, you'll be seeing a lot more of him from now on." Gretel's lips were still pressed together, but her eyes were dancing.

"He's buying a house right here in Illustria."

"You're kidding. That's amazing!"

"Yeah, some crazy rock-star mansion out east, weirdly close to the Deadwoods for my taste… You know what he's like. Anyway, I guess it's safe again out there these days, even in the Forbidden Triangle. The Whispering trees are being cut down and replaced with regular ones. Our best Magiscientists are at work undoing all the evil enchantments one by one, wherever they're found. The Piper was flattened by Golden Thunder's egg-bomb." Gretel took a deep breath. "And, most important of all, the witch is dead. She didn't get a chance to magic her way out of that oven before the egg fell on the cottage. All thanks to you."

This was the closest Roxy was ever going to get to praise from her sister, and she knew it.

"Thanks, Gretel," she said.

"And Han wants you to go and stay with him whenever you want … we both want you to go and stay whenever you want … not that I'm trying to get rid of you, Roxy, you understand?" Colour was appearing in Gretel's cheeks. She cleared her throat and fussed with the strings on Roxy's hoodie, trying to make them level. "You do know that when Han and I were saying you weren't important, I only meant you weren't important *to the Gingerbread Witch*. Which meant that you were safe. At least, you would have been, if you hadn't gone waltzing right into the heart of her territory." Her cheeks were now the colour of her coat. "And when I said you were silly and childish … well, OK, I *did* think you were a bit of a silly kid, but that was my mistake, Roxy, and—"

"Gretel. It's OK." Roxy did not want to go over (and over) all the stuff they'd already talked about that night that Golden Thunder had flown them out of the Deadwoods. "I get it. I'm just glad I could help."

"ROXYYYYY! Get a blooming move on!" This was Jones, beckoning to her from across the courtyard.

"Go and see Golden Thunder," said Gretel, already turning and disappearing back through the door she had appeared from. "I'll see you in the throne room for the ceremony. *Please* try and tidy up your hair beforehand. And I know you think it's embarrassing –" she turned back, giving a brisk wave – "but I for one am proud of you."

This gave Roxy a toasty-warm feeling, from head to toe, that reminded her of the way the Grit had felt in her palm just before she had used it to do magic. Or rather, as she now knew, just before she had done magic *all by herself*, with the Grit merely channelling it for her. It was weird to think that she was part magical – so weird that she was trying to think about it *as little as possible* – but she couldn't deny, it had its advantages.

A deafening CHEEEEP! made Roxy jump as she hurried after the others. It was coming from the stable block, which was quite unlike any stable block Roxy had ever seen before. Not only was it made of actual marble with a beautiful gold-tiled roof, but it was absolutely vast: the height and breadth of at least a couple of double-decker buses. A mound of bright-yellow fluff was protruding from one of the windows.

"Doesn't she look amazing?" Jones was saying, as Roxy puffed in. She and Charmian were stroking Golden Thunder's huge orange beak, as the giant baby chick ducked her head in appreciation.

"She does. She really does. Hi, Golden Thunder." Roxy reached up to stroke her beak too. "We've missed you!"

"There's someone else for you to catch up with, too," Charley said, squeezing round the chick's wings to duck into a small office tucked at the back of the stall. A moment later, he appeared again, followed by Susan-Bedelia Little.

"Susan!" Jones hauled the huge woman out from behind Golden Thunder. "What are you doing here?"

"Girls. Ah, and Frankie, too." Susan Little nodded, briskly, at them all. She was still wearing her wolfskin cloak and, thanks to the warmer weather here in Illustria, was looking rather sweaty. "Getting to know each other?"

"Oh, we know each other from way back." Frankie beamed, linking her arm through Roxy's. "Susan-Bedelia is my brand-new colleague," she told her, in a gossiping tone. "She's specializing in designing tracking equipment for Golden Thunder to use on all sorts of exciting missions. After all, now that magic is no longer banned in Illustria... Oh, no! There I go again!"

Jones and Roxy turned to stare at Jones's fairy godmother.

"You're kidding me?" Jones was the first to speak. "The Ministry is *no longer banning magic*?"

"Oh, it's better than that!" blurted Frankie, excitedly. "They're going to lift the False Memory Enchantment, too! Well, there's absolutely no way the rest of the Missing children can ever go home other-wise – think of poor dear Sam – and Queen Ariadne has insisted that it's unfair, if *she* gets her children back, that other families in Illustria don't--"

"Good to know you were paying attention in all those *top-secret* meetings," Susan said, pointedly. "But yes, Frankie -- or rather, Illustria's brand-new Deputy Assistant Chief of Charm Reversal – is correct," she said. "The False Memory Enchantment is going to be lifted, and the magic ban along with it. My colleagues at SkyZone are confident that Diabolical Magic has been so thoroughly and irreversibly weakened – thanks to you chaps! – that the Ministry is just working out how to banish all the restrictions. A few more months –" she turned to pat Golden Thunder between the eyes – "and this gorgeous girl will be out and about in the skies above Illustria, performing all sorts of important tasks."

"Her first task will be to fly all the Missing kids back down from SkyZone," Charley added, with the air of a person who has been in on a secret for weeks and can't wait to spill the beans. "Sam's going to come and visit me at the Palace as soon as he's allowed. He's already asked his parents. Everyone in SkyZone has had visits from their families now. Bet *that* was an amazing day up there."

"And Susan's designing special tracking equipment so that GT can be used for magical-object recovery all over the world!" Charmian joined in, before Charley carried on where she left off, so seamlessly that it was as if one person was talking rather than two: "Mum wants to set up a museum, you see, of all the magical artefacts from the Cursed Kingdom that BOBIs might have taken with them when they left…"

"That reminds me!" Susan slapped a hand to her forehead. "Magical objects!" She disappeared into her office for a moment, then reappeared with something under her arm, wrapped in black velvet cloth. "OK, so when I was finally allowed back to my cabin," she began, "I started trying to collect up all the things that Golden Thunder had accidentally flung out of my workshop when she smashed through the roof. And that's when I found Mirror. Or rather, that's when I found Mirror's frame, and nineteen thousand eight hundred and fifty-four shards of shattered glass. I know the exact number," she went on, starting to unwrap the black cloth, "because my brilliant Magiscientist friend Letty who works in the Fixing Magical Objects department at SkyZone told me, after she'd put them all back together again…"

She held out a perfectly whole – though just as tarnished as usual – Mirror.

"It's me!" shrieked Mirror, as Roxy gathered it into her arms, speechless with joy. "I'm back! They fixed my glass! I'm really super-well!"

"Oh, no. Here we go again," groaned Jones.

"And VERY NICE TO SEE YOU, TOO!" Mirror huffed.

"It's OK, Mirror. Jones loves you really." Roxy hugged Mirror tightly to her chest. "Don't you,

Jones?"

Jones rolled her eyes.

"*Jones*," said Roxy, meaningfully.

"Oh, all right!" Jones let out a long sigh, then finally reached out to give Mirror a little rub on its discoloured silver frame. "I'm actually really glad to see you, Mirror."

"You are? I couldn't tell," sniffed Mirror.

"OK, don't push it—"

"There's going to be a special place for Mirror in Queen Ariadne's brand-new exhibition of Enchanted Objects," Susan interrupted Jones, "and after that, it can choose whichever room in the Palace it wants to live in."

"I'm thinking that the *ballroom* might be quite the place to be!" Mirror sounded excited. "Or Ariadne's dressing room... We'll simply have to see."

"Yeah, well, as long as you don't end up in Charley's bedroom," said Jones. "I wouldn't want you to get worn out from overuse, Mirror."

"Hey, when you're as good-looking as I am, you don't *need* to check out your reflection every five minutes," said Charley, as his sister stifled a snort.

"Could your head *get* any bigger?" scoffed Jones.

"Could *your* head get any smaller?" replied Charley.

"Could your—"

## "CHEEEEP!"

"Quite right too, Golden Thunder." Roxy patted the chick. "I think we've all had enough of their bickering."

"It's not just that," said Susan. "Golden Thunder needs to go out for her mid-morning flight. She gets ever so cranky without regular exercise."

"Can we take her?" Jones begged, as Susan pressed a button that slid back the stable roof, ready for lift-off. "Please?"

"I suppose…"

"Awesome!" Jones didn't give Susan time to think twice about it; she was already swinging herself up onto Golden Thunder's back. "You're coming too, Roxy, right?"

Roxy had no intention of thinking twice herself, and she handed Mirror carefully to Frankie before scrambling up behind her friend. "Do you want to come?" she asked Charley and Charmian.

The twins glanced at each other before Charley spoke for them both.

"Nah." He grinned and shook his head. "You should go by yourselves. Besides, it's not like we don't have a million other opportunities to take her for a spin," he added, unable to resist winding Jones up one more time. "You know, what with living here full time in this amazing Royal Palace..."

Jones reached down and slipped off her boot, which was already loose, and flung it at Charley's head as Golden Thunder began to rise up out of the stable.

"Bye, guys!" whooped Charmian, punching the air. "Do a loop-the-loop for me!"

"No looping any loops!" Frankie shrieked, through cupped hands. "And don't be too long! Don't you girls have medals to collect in fifteen minutes?"

"Relax, Frankie! Anyway, Queen Ariadne will wait for us, right?"

"You know what, Jones? I don't actually think she will," Roxy broke it to her. "I mean, she's kind of top dog around here."

"Yeah, well, we'll see about that..." Jones hung on tight to Golden Thunder's yellow fluff as the chick began to soar upwards. "Let's face it, she's won't be able to get crabby with the people who brought her kids back. *Or* with her new Head Organizer for the Magical Objects of the Cursed Kingdom exhibition."

"Sorry – who *is* the new Head Organizer for the Magical Objects of the Cursed Kingdom exhibition?" asked Roxy.

"Me, of course!" Jones said. "Well, it *will* be. I haven't actually applied for the job yet."

"But don't you have to be...?" Roxy gave up. There was no point telling Jones that she was not old enough, or that she might need official qualifications, or anything else, for that matter. If Jones wanted this job, Jones would get it. There could be absolutely no doubt about that. "Well, congratulations on the new job, Jones. You deserve it."

"And I'll need a part-time assistant, obviously," Jones said, off-handedly, "especially when I'm out there actually *finding* the magical objects. Preferably a person that can do a bit of magic. That'd come in pretty handy."

"No problem, Jones." Roxy smiled at her friend's reluctance to actually ask her outright. She put her hand, briefly, on Jones's shoulder. "I'm with you."

Just for a moment, Jones lifted her hand to squeeze Roxy's. "I was wondering," she went on, quickly, "if Charmian was serious about us doing that loop-the-loop? I mean, we've never tried one before, but..."

Roxy gazed down at the peaceful city below.

"Well," she said, "there's a first time for everything, right?"

"Right!" whooped Jones.

"CHEEP," agreed Golden Thunder.

"Then let's do this," said Roxy, holding on tightly as

Jones spurred the giant chick onwards and upwards. It was going to be another exciting ride.

# ACKNOWLEDGEMENTS

Enormous thanks are owed to the amazing and eagle-eyed Emma Lidbury and all the fabulous team at Walker – their patience and humour know no bounds! And enormous thanks, too, to the incomparable Helen Boyle, aka (to her lucky clients) SuperAgent, with whom the strangest conversations about giant chicks seem reassuringly normal. Huge gratitude to R and SL, and as always to Josh, who bravely and cheerfully took over homeschooling to allow me to FINISH. And, of course, to Lara, who accompanied me on many, many Story Walks and continues to allow me to "borrow" most of her best ideas.

**Angela Woolfe** is the author of the Avril Crump trilogy as well as a series of magical adventures for younger readers under the pseudonym Emerald Everheart. This is her second book about the inimitable Roxy and Jones, and follows on from their adventures in *Roxy & Jones: The Great Fairytale Cover-Up*. She is married with one young daughter, who is even more obsessed with fairytales than she is. Angela lives in Wimbledon.